GREEN SHOOTS

AN ECO-THRILLER

BEN WESTWOOD

CRANTHORPE
MILLNER

First published by Cranthorpe Millner Publishers (2022)

ISBN 978-1-80378-045-0 (Paperback)

www.cranthorpemillner.com

Cranthorpe Millner Publishers

About the author

Ben Westwood is an author, lecturer and performer. He has worked for many years as a journalist, writing for publications including The Daily Telegraph, The Times, The Guardian and The Independent. He lived for several years in South America and has authored travel guidebooks to Ecuador, Galapagos and Peru. Ben now lives in East Sussex with his two children and lectures at the University of Brighton. In his spare time, he is a singer-songwriter and has released two self-funded albums. Green Shoots is his first novel and draws on his own experience of grief and of living in Ecuador. See benwestwood.net for further information.

For Carolina, Jake and Isabella

One impulse from a vernal wood
May teach you more of man,
Of moral evil and of good,
Than all the sages can.

Sweet is the lore which Nature brings;
Our meddling intellect
Mis-shapes the beauteous forms
of things:—
We murder to dissect.

The Tables Turned, William Wordsworth

Chapter 1

I'm not sure I believe in heaven. I'm not sure I believe in anything anymore. I remember you used to tell me there was enough heaven on Earth to enjoy and that settled it. But you're not on Earth anymore, so what's left for me here?

If I believed in heaven, I'd have to believe you're up there watching over me. But if you could see me like this, surely that would be hell for you.

I'm parked on a grass verge with the engine running. About fifty feet ahead of me through the fog, the land gives way to the cliff face. I can see the faint glow from the Beachy Head lighthouse below. It's hidden in the night, but oblivion is close.

You always hated this car. I went for the safe option. I should enjoy the irony of smashing to bits the car you never liked. I would if I had any joy left. You wouldn't want me smashed to bits though. You'd want me to keep going. But for what?

I talk to you but I don't know if you're there. I don't want you to be there anyway, watching me put my foot on the accelerator and drive the car until it runs out of earth, falling through air into darkness.

I count the seconds: 1, 2, 3, 4, 5... that's how long it will take the car to fall five hundred feet – five seconds. I did my research. If my life flashes before my eyes, I want your face to be the last thing I see – the way you used to tilt your head to the side smiling at me.

I close my eyes to see you beckoning. All I have to do is press the pedal and let the car do the rest. I lean on the accelerator and the engine growls. I look at the clock on the dashboard: 1.59 a.m. I feel a gnawing in my gut. Part of me doesn't want it to reach the hour mark.

Then I hear something out of place. A piano and drums. My phone is ringing. Who would be calling me now? Private number. I press reject. Just leave me in peace.

I look at my phone, the screensaver of me kissing your cheek at the airport the day you left. I'd give anything to go back to that day. I stare at the photograph, at you smiling at me, imprinting your image on my mind.

My phone vibrates. A message appears: "Don't do it, John. Turn off the engine."

I freeze, re-reading it. Is someone watching me? I turn around to look through the gloom. An empty road, fog hiding the Downs. My foot is still on the pedal.

Suddenly, there are flashing blue lights behind me. A sharp knock on the window. "Sir, are you okay in there?" A flashlight blinds me but I glimpse a police uniform.

She lowers the torch and leans in. "Not going to do anything silly, are we?"

I don't know how to respond.

"Sir, for your own safety, please step out of the vehicle and hand me the keys."

I hesitate, then the car door flies open and a hand reaches in and snatches the keys.

I get out of the car in a daze. She asks for my licence. "Have you been drinking, sir?" She nods at the bottle of brandy on the passenger seat.

"No, not really. I don't remember."

I'm in the back of a police car. We drive along backroads I don't recognise, and I wonder how long until we reach the police station. I've never been in trouble with the law. I report on crime, I don't commit crimes. I wasn't looking to collect new experiences tonight though. This was to be my last night on Earth, not a first night in a police cell.

The fog is thick through the car window. A heavy fatigue creeps over me. I lean back on the headrest and close my eyes.

***

I'm at the hospital in Ecuador. A battered, faded yellow building with paint peeling off the walls. It's so hot. My shirt is drenched, sticking to my backbone. A shrill alarm bell pierces my ear drums. I'm running down the corridor, desperately looking for the right department. The sun is beating down. I look up squinting to see the hospital has no roof.

"Christina Bautista, dónde?" I struggle for the Spanish for intensive care. The nurse ignores me. Stupid *gringo*.

I keep running, but the corridor is like a conveyor belt against me. I'm lost. There's a little girl playing on a plastic slide with a group of children. They look at me, pointing and laughing. What are they doing here?

"John, where are you?" I hear Christina's voice coming from the end of the corridor. I can see her through the glass. She rolls her eyes at me as if to say, "John, late again." I smile and shrug, relieved, but her eyes roll up into the back of her head and she shakes violently.

"Christina, no, wait! I'm here!"

Her body goes limp. The nurse takes her pulse, then looks at me with hatred and shakes her head.

Stupid *gringo*. It's all my fault.

***

I wake up, struggling to breathe. I've had the same nightmare for months. Worse than a nightmare, as it's so close to the truth.

I'm on my side of the bed, a habit that's hard to break. There's a split second every morning when I reach over as I always did. Part of me hopes to feel Christina's body, to see her face. It's the best split second of the day, but her side is always empty. I don't know why I don't pack her pillow away. Well, I do know why.

Memories of last night are blurry. I lose hours sometimes, but I remember I wasn't expecting to see another morning in this flat, the flat we bought together and where we planned to start a family. We had the extra bedroom, but I persuaded Christina to wait until she'd finished her research. It seemed like a good plan, until she went to the jungle.

I look at the clock: past midday. At least I don't have to wonder what to do with the morning. I used to wake up to the smell of fresh coffee. Christina was usually up before me and said it wasn't a good morning without coffee. No coffee aroma today though, just my musty pillow that needs washing.

My phone is ringing. I pick it up from the bedside table. It's Steve checking up on me, as he does several times a week.

"Hey, buddy, good to see you're up early." His humour used to make me laugh, but not so much now.

I play along though, like an actor delivering well-rehearsed lines. "Before two p.m., not bad going."

I feel a ripple of guilt. Steve has no idea what I nearly did last night.

"Listen, John, the editor said take as much time as you need. It's up to you when you feel like getting back in the saddle, but a package arrived today addressed to you, marked private and confidential."

Nothing extraordinary about that. People often send confidential information to the crime desk.

"We opened it, mate. Figured it might be a story."

"What was in it?"

"A USB, encrypted though. We couldn't open it and thought you might have a go."

I rub my forehead. "Steve, I can barely get up, let alone work."

"I get that, but it could help to sniff out a story again. How about I courier it across? Take a look, that's all. No pressure."

Steve is a good friend and a great reporter. He means well, so it's easier to tell him what he wants to hear.

"Okay, but no promises."

"Understood. And, buddy, let's have a drink soon when you're up to it."

Steve doesn't know that drinking is the one thing I haven't stopped since Christina died.

Chapter 2: Blakely

Blakely took his usual seat at the bar. He was here most nights from about seven p.m. – a comforting routine for a high-functioning alcoholic. Another long day at the office, but days were getting tougher. The company was becoming more demanding since the Latin American partnership took off. Loose ends to tie up, transactions to complete and tracks to cover to keep the bosses happy. That part was more exhausting than the hours.

Blakely used to drive home to his five-bedroom house on the edge of Hampstead Heath and tell himself it was worth it, but now he wasn't so sure. His wife had left when it became clear she was a distant third behind the company and the bottle. Now he lived in a house with too many empty rooms.

He loved this bar though. The oak tables and the finest selection of single malts in London. The dim lighting helped hide the shadows under his eyes, and the whisky relieved the weight on his shoulders. Jack was a good bartender too. He could tell Jack about his day – the parts he could talk about – and he seemed genuinely interested, but there was a new guy tonight.

"Where's Jack?"

"Taking the night off," replied the bartender. "Family bereavement, I believe."

"Oh, sorry to hear that."

There had been too much death recently. The bar seemed emptier than usual. Sometimes he could tap into the laughter of fellow patrons and go home persuading himself it wasn't such a bad life. He might have to get deeper into the drink tonight, so he ordered a bottle of GlenDronach Parliament 21.

The bartender hesitated before replying, "I'm sorry, sir, we only serve full bottles to groups. New bar policy."

Blood rushed to Blakely's face. "Who brought that policy in? Jack never said no."

"I'm very sorry, sir. I don't make the rules. We're trying to look after our customers. I can serve you that malt by the shot though."

Blakely got angry. "Don't patronise me. I'm a bloody patron here! Give me a triple shot then – for starters."

A tall, dark-haired man took the stool next to Blakely. The barman gave him a faint nod. He adjusted his thick glasses and turned to Blakely. "I'll share a bottle with you if you like," he said, offering his hand. Blakely hesitated before shaking it, hiding his discomfort at the bone-crushing grip.

The man glanced with casual confidence at the barman: "Will a group of two suffice?" The barman regarded him stiffly before setting out the bottle and glasses.

It was a great malt. The 'finest Scotch south of the border', the bar claimed, and it wasn't just marketing guff. His new drinking partner introduced himself only as Bill. They began chatting and Blakely thought the evening was turning out better than expected. Bill knew a lot about finance. He was keen to know more about the company's new ventures in South America though, and that made Blakely uneasy. After all, he wanted to forget all that for a few hours.

Bill was bulky and, judging by his biceps when he took off his jacket, he worked out regularly. He told Blakely he ran a hedge fund and offered to run a few investment opportunities past him. It sounded of interest. As Blakely turned and rummaged in his pocket for a business card, for a second he thought he saw Bill touch his glass. Perhaps he'd imagined it.

Bill didn't seem to be drinking much whisky; his glass was still half full when he poured Blakely another shot. As a numbness spread through Blakely's limbs, he wondered if getting so drunk was a good idea when he had an important meeting in the morning.

His vision began to blur. The room was spinning. Bill took out his phone under the bar, sent a text and put it back in his pocket. He turned to bleary-eyed Blakely and suggested they get some air. Blakely felt in no state to argue.

Two businessmen worse for wear seemed far from

unusual in this bar, so the other customers paid little attention when Bill half-carried Blakely to the back.

The barman concentrated on cleaning glasses, keeping his gaze down as the two men stumbled out of the fire escape and into an alleyway where a car was waiting.

Chapter 3

The details of last night are coming back. I was at Beachy Head, I know that much. I should have known there would be police patrols at such a notorious spot.

They were nice officers actually. They breathalysed me at the station, but it came up clear and then things got more relaxed. They insisted on a brief chat with a counsellor though. It must have been past five a.m. when I arrived home.

I get out of bed, open the curtains and look down at the street. My car isn't there. Now I remember – the police called me a taxi back to London. They probably thought I might drive my car back up to the cliff edge. They were probably right. I need to go back and collect my car from Eastbourne. That's a pain.

Lucky the police arrived when they did. But was it lucky? Waking up to yet another day alone in this flat doesn't feel much like good luck.

I'd forgotten about the phone call. I lean over and check my call history. A private number called at 1.59 a.m., and there's the text message. So I didn't imagine it. Someone tried to talk me out of it last night, but who?

There's a knock at the door. I get off the bed, go into the hall and look through the spyhole. A dispatch uniform. That was quick. I sign for a brown A4 envelope, addressed to John Adamson, Crime Desk, *The Sentinel*.

Inside, I find a small wooden box, and inside that an oblong wooden stick that must be the USB. I hold it in my hand, deliberating. Part of me is intrigued, but most of me is just very tired.

I cross over to the shelf to find my laptop. It's dusty, unused for weeks. The USB is password protected, so I press the password hint option. It reads: 'Last night's deadly beauty spot.'

I jump back from the screen, staring at the cursor. Whoever sent this USB knows where I was last night.

I put in 'beachyhead'. Incorrect. I try 'Beachy Head' and it opens.

There's a folder called 'Blakely'. Inside are photos of a car. It looks like the interior of a garage. There's a hose through the driver's window and close-ups of a man, clearly dead. He's approaching middle age, judging from the thinning hair. I've seen enough bodies in my line of work, so it's hardly a shock.

Another photograph shows a single word, written in smudged black on the windscreen: 'Oil.'

There's a document on the passenger seat. It looks like a printout of a newswire: 'Mysterious deaths of indigenous leaders resisting oil drilling in Ecuador.'

Ecuador – Christina's country, and where she died.

I skim the article. The indigenous leaders were found at the bottom of a ravine.

The last photograph is also on the passenger seat. It's some kind of mural. On the left is a scene of scorched earth, blackened tree stumps, skulls and bones, merging into thick forest on the right with toucans, monkeys and indigenous children.

The graffiti written in white in the soil below reads: '*De sus cenizas, crecerán brotes verdes.*' My Spanish is good enough to know it means: 'Out of their ashes, green shoots will grow.' I stare at the mural, repeating the words. It's beautiful but troubling.

The old me would be fascinated to receive this information, but my head is pounding. I don't know what any of this means, who sent the flash drive or how the hell they knew where I was last night.

My phone rings. Private number. I need to answer it this time.

"Hello, John. How are you feeling today?"

"Who is this? How did you get my number?"

"Relax, I mean you no harm. Otherwise, I'd have told you to step on the gas last night, not stop."

So this is the man that sent me that text. His voice is slow, like he's choosing every word carefully. There's a hint of transatlantic to his accent. I can't place it.

"Have you been watching me?"

"That doesn't matter right now. What matters is you have work to do if you want to find out what really happened to your wife."

"What *really* happened? What the hell do you know about my wife?"

"All in good time, John. I won't say you owe me your life, but you do owe me a favour. That's how this works. I want you to look into this."

"Look into what?"

"Blakely worked in oil. A lot happening in Ecuador in that industry. Christina knew that. There may be connections. Her blog might shed some light."

He pauses while I take this in. I knew Christina had a blog, but shed light on what?

"Read it more closely, John, and join the dots. I'll give you more when you've looked into this case. Quid pro quo."

"I want to know who I'm talking to."

"A private investigator and an interested party. Call me Root."

The phone goes dead.

14

Chapter 4

The London media is in shock today after the sudden death of award-winning journalist John Bautista Adamson, aged 37. He was found in a car wreck at the foot of notorious suicide spot Beachy Head yesterday.

John Adamson grew up in Sussex and studied English at UCL. He began a PHD on the poetry of TS Eliot but left to pursue journalism. After two years as a regional reporter, John specialised in crime and joined The Sentinel. *He won British Journalism Awards for investigations on the Stephen Lawrence case and an undercover investigation of a London crime syndicate, which led to him receiving police protection.*

John met his wife Christina Bautista in Ecuador in 2016, marrying her the following year. However, tragedy struck when Christina died in October last year of a tropical disease while doing research in Ecuador. John was devoted to his wife and deeply affected by her passing. His death comes four months later. The couple had no children.

I've been lying in bed, composing that obituary in my head. Self-indulgence, I know. At least I made my mark, but would it all come to an end at the bottom of a cliff? It nearly did. Part of me still wishes it had.

I've hardly got out of bed for days. At one point I thought the floor was shaking. It was ages before I realised it was in fact me that was shaking. I think it was tremors, most likely caused by stress, according to the doctor. I'm in a bad way, that's for sure.

I need to get my head together. If I can deal with threats from crime syndicates, surely I can deal with being stalked by a private snoop, if that's what this guy is. He did try to talk me off a cliff edge though, so I must be worth more to him alive than dead.

I decide to take a shower. Personal hygiene is one of many things I've let slip recently. Water usually relaxes me and clears my head, but every inch of this flat reminds me of Christina, even the rainmaker cubicle we installed. Standing inside, I close my eyes and can almost see the curves of her body, feel her lips pressed against me. The memory takes me back for a moment, until I catch sight of myself in the bathroom mirror, naked and alone. It's pathetic.

I open the wardrobe to pick out something other than the sweatpants and t-shirt I've been living in for weeks. It's still divided into our two sides. That embroidered blue dress Christina bought from Otavalo market in Ecuador. I press it to my face and inhale. There's still a hint of her perfume: her favourite *Gio*. I shudder to think

I used to moan it was too expensive. Now it's priceless. I will never get rid of that dress for fear of losing the scent of her.

Is it perfume from a dress that makes me so digress?

Something is nagging me. Something I've forgotten. I've always prided myself on my memory, especially in my job: recalling and transcribing entire sentences of conversations without a recording. My memory has really failed me recently though. The other week I even lost my phone for a few days, only to find it in my car. At least I hadn't already ordered a new one, but I still can't work out how my phone got there, as I hadn't driven the car in weeks.

Now I remember – what this 'Root' said on the phone: "What *really* happened to your wife." He mentioned Christina's blog. I need to find out what he meant. I remember Christina sent me a blog link a few weeks into her trip. I read some of the posts but she asked me not to comment much until it was finished and then I could edit it. I couldn't bear to read it at all after she died.

She named the blog 'Chrissy Baños' after the place where we first met in Ecuador. We used to joke that we couldn't have picked a more sinister date to meet: 6th June – 6/6. "The day I met my English devil!" she would say, and I'd reply, "And you've been in hot water ever since!" It was our in-joke because we met in the thermal baths in the mountain town Baños. The front page of her blog has a picture of those baths. I thought that was

17

sweet of her, but looking at it now is unbearable.

It's going to take time to read through it all because there are over a dozen posts. I start at the top with the final post.

More troubles in paradise

Today I saw more evidence of extraction on the Aguarico. I asked to come along on an excursion with the men. They were reluctant at first – maybe they didn't think it was a trip for a woman. Sometimes their old-fashioned ways are endearing, sometimes a little annoying, but they seemed concerned for my safety.

We went a few miles upstream to an area I'd visited a few weeks before. They took spears with them, which made me uneasy. We approached a long mud bank where I think we disembarked before, but I couldn't be sure because the change to the area was shocking. Previously, there had been dense forest overhanging the tributaries, teeming with wildlife, but now the landscape was dominated by a large yellow digger on the embankment. It looked so out of place, like a giant wasp. Trees had been cut down and a track carved from the river bank through the forest, likely connecting to a main road. They are building deeper into the jungle, and as soon as the machines come, the wildlife disappears.

There were no miners, which was a relief. I didn't want to get caught up in a fight, and the men were visibly angry. They chatted away in Kichwa, pointing and shaking their heads. They believe that for every tree cut down, the forest loses a part of its soul and the tree spirits flee. Because the villagers believe they are one with the forest, they lose part of their soul too.

I hate mining. I will never wear gold again now I've seen the price the forest pays for its extraction. The worst problem for locals is the mercury that poisons the river and drinking supply, leaving many of them with kidney failure or brain damage. Now I realise that the problems I've seen in many of the children are not genetic at all.

The mining companies deny using mercury or claim it's used at safe levels, but I don't believe a word. Looking at the muddy pool dug into the riverbank and a black pipe snaking down to the Aguarico, I wondered if the poison had spread downstream to the village, into the water used for cooking, and into my water bottle.

I feel so powerless. The might of mining is daunting. How do we stop this? All I can do is note down what I see and write about it.

Nobody talked on the way back to the village.

The post ends there. I knew Christina was researching ecotourism and community projects. She was excited by her research and travelled to Ecuador to document examples of good practice. It looks like she found a very different situation to what she'd expected though. I wish I'd taken a closer interest in her research. Just one of my regrets.

I scroll through and read several supportive comments on the blog post. The last two comments stand out, from a user named *Chelomimi2000*.

Ten cuidado, Señora Bautista. Que dios te protega – 'Be careful. May God protect you.'

The comment is dated 4th October, the day after her post was published and a week before Christina died. It reads like a warning, or a threat.

The final comment on the blog post is from the same user: *Paz en su tumba –* 'Peace in your tomb.' The equivalent of 'rest in peace', but it sounds more sinister to me in Spanish. Next to the comment is an uploaded photograph of a single white cross. It's dated 12th October, the day after Christina died.

I stare at the screen. It's like I'm back in the hospital again, falling. The man on the phone may be right and something else entirely happened to my wife. If so, I have to find out who did this to her, who did this to us.

"Join the dots," he said.

I'm shaking again. I feel something I haven't felt in a long time – anger.

I have work to do.

Chapter 5: Grover

Grover woke up to a faint sound of music. Fear crept up his spine. When the music started, that meant *he* was back. He heard rats scampering away. They gave him no rest when he was alone. In the dark under the blindfold, he couldn't see how close they were. It might almost be worth it to suffer them crawling on him if they would only gnaw away the ropes that bound him.

The music grew louder. There was whispering and an ominous bass. He thought he heard the words "three days". Grover wondered if it was a message. Had he been here for three days? He remembered two long periods of total darkness.

A flicker of light under the blindfold indicated movement. This man moved so silently, it was unnerving. Grover jumped as a hand slapped him on the shoulder. "Relax, Jeremy, we got what we needed."

He seemed happy. There was hope. "Then you'll let me go? You said if I did as you asked…"

He felt ropes untied and a hand under his arm. "Up on your feet." He crumpled almost as soon as he stood.

He'd been tied to the chair so long, his legs were weak.

"Come on, Jeremy. Can I call you Jerry? How can you go if you can't even stand?"

"Oh, thank God."

"God has nothing to do with it. Just one more thing I need you to do. Up on the step!"

Grover's hands were still tied behind his back. He felt his foot on a step, then the other foot. Three steps, then he stopped.

"Are we going upstairs?"

A soft laugh. "I think you might be going downstairs actually, although I don't really believe in that. Do you, Jerry?"

As Grover wondered what that meant, he felt something pass over his head and around his neck. Hope drained as quickly as it had emerged.

"You said you'd let me go!"

"I would have thought an accountant like yourself would pay closer attention to detail, Jerry. I said you would be free. Free of your burdens. Now hush, there's something I want you to see."

His blindfold was removed. In front of him was a screen showing a video of a forest with a large tree at the centre.

"What is this?" Grover pleaded, trying to turn around, but he was restricted by the rope around his neck. He couldn't see anyone. He'd never seen him, even when he was hit over the head walking home.

"I thought you'd recognise this scene. After all,

you've made a lot of money from it."

He broke off to sing along to the music, which was building to a crescendo.

"This is the kapok tree, known in South America as the 'ceiba' tree. It's considered sacred. It grows over 200 feet high and lives for many centuries."

He continued. "It gives life to hundreds of species but the wood is of the highest quality, as you know well. It takes a lot of time and effort to bring down such a tree. You must be proud of such efficient work."

Grover could hear the high-pitched whirr of machinery on the video.

"What? This isn't my work. I import sustainable timber."

A sarcastic laugh. "Sustainable? Yes, I'm sure you check every shipment carefully to ensure it complies."

He interrupted Grover's protests. "The kapok is considered a god of the forest. Do you know what happens when you destroy a god of the forest, Jeremy?"

Grover pleaded, "No! Look, I'll leave my job, anything you want. I'm sorry, just let me go."

"Too late. If you destroy the god of the forest, you are cursed forever. Our fate is tied to that of the trees, you see. *Your* fate is tied to this particular tree, Jerry. So watch carefully."

The noise of the machinery grew louder. There was an excruciating creak as the trunk of the tree began to split.

"Any last words?"

Grover opened his mouth, but he had nothing. He stared transfixed as the huge kapok tree began to lean.

"Suit yourself. Here's one word for you: timber!" He broke into a hollow laugh.

The stepladder was kicked away and the noose dug into Grover's neck as his legs kicked at the air. The timber beam creaked above his head.

The great kapok tree leaned and fell with a shattering crash as Grover choked. Their fates entwined, until both were no more.

Chapter 6

My phone buzzes. A text message from a private number: 'Check your work email.'

It must be him. So we're on email terms now. "No more USBs?" I say out loud, half expecting someone to answer.

It's easy enough to find out my email address, as newspaper accounts follow the same format. I open it on the laptop; there are a hundred and sixty-three unread messages. I have some catching up to do, or maybe I should just delete them all. Most will be out-of-date press releases or invitations I don't want.

The latest message is from the email address 'squareroot64'. He's dispensed with using the password-protected encryption then. The email has a zip file of photographs, named 'Surrey swingers'. Something tells me this isn't from a middle-class swingers club in leafy Surrey.

I open the first photo and instantly regret it. There's a dead man hanging. The light is poor – a relief in a way because I can't see his agonised expression too clearly.

He's wearing a shirt and tie. Beneath him is a step ladder lying on the floor. It looks like he's in a warehouse, but it's too dark to be sure.

'Surrey swingers' – this guy really has a sick sense of humour. I feel the need to breathe. Starved of oxygen, I've always thought hanging is a terrible way to die, unless it's done properly and breaks the neck. Using a stepladder, that would be highly unlikely. This would have been slow.

Looking at the photo reminds me why I chose a cliff edge over a noose. Or nearly did. I suppose the chances of the police interrupting hanging are far smaller.

The second photo: 'Out of their ashes, green shoots will grow.' The words are scratched into wood. The same message but in English this time. It looks a lot more sinister than the mural. The rope is just visible in the corner of the photo so it must be carved into the beam he's hanging from.

The third photo shows a single word: 'Timber.' It appears to be written in wood shavings on top of a table.

On the same table, there's a document. I zoom in and see a report with the headline: 'The deadly cost of timber.' At first glance, it's an exposé of illegal logging in South America. It mentions the impunity that leads to illegal wood ending up on European markets.

So now we've got two dead businessmen. Both look like suicide, but they're clearly linked because similar messages were found with the bodies. I don't know who the dead man is but I'm betting he had some involvement in timber. First oil, now timber – both raw materials sold by far from scrupulous companies. Is this a bizarre suicide pact? Somehow, I doubt it.

The zip file name isn't just black humour, it's a clue to where this happened. I check the Surrey police website and find a report from today. 'Missing man found dead in warehouse.' The victim is named Jeremy Grover. He'd been missing for a week when his body was found in an abandoned warehouse a few miles outside Guildford. The police are appealing for information.

I check the Met's press releases but there's nothing on Blakely. Different police forces, so the Met and Surrey police may not have made a connection between the cases. My best contact at the Met is Detective Chief Inspector Denise Morrison, so I give her a call.

"Hello, Denise, long time no speak."

"John, it's been a while. I heard you were on leave. Back to the grind then?"

I'm guessing from her upbeat tone she has no idea why I took leave. It's a welcome relief. I'm sick of people treating me like a lame puppy.

"Yes, getting back to it. I wanted to ask about Keith Blakely. He was found dead in his car last week?"

"You boys are keen on this one, aren't you? A colleague of yours – Rupert, wasn't it? – he asked about it too. One of your protégés, is he?"

That annoys me. Rupert Hennessy is no protégé of mine. Steve must have passed him the case. He's been filling in for me at the paper and is clearly after my job, the little trust fund twat. Only been out of Cambridge a couple of years and thinks he's brilliant.

I hear Morrison typing as she brings up the file. "Keith Blakely, 42, found in Hampstead. Evidence points to suicide but not confirmed. Heavy drinker, recently divorced. We're still waiting for the tox screen to come back though."

DCI Morrison is a tough customer and works very hard. She doesn't take any crap either after years muscling into a boys club like the Met. We've always got along and there's mutual respect.

She continues. "There are a few loose ends though. Last seen Thursday night, emailed in sick Friday morning, according to the company he worked for, Anglo-American Petrol. Not found until the following Tuesday morning, but initial pathology estimates he'd only been dead a few hours when he was found in his garage."

That leaves three days unaccounted for.

"I understand there were papers and a message found with the body. Is it correct that the word 'oil' was written on the windscreen?"

"How do you know that, John? As far as I know, it wasn't released to the press."

"Anonymous tip-off. Denise, you know me better than to ask my sources."

"Hmm, well it was his fingerprint and there was oil on his index. A one-word suicide note is unusual but who knows what goes on in people's minds if they're in that state?"

I wince at that. Yes, who knows.

"On a related note, have you been in touch with Surrey about Jeremy Grover? The similarities between the cases are striking."

She puts me on hold for a few minutes. It seems I was right and the police forces haven't made a connection yet.

She comes back on the line. "John, which similarities are you referring to?"

"Both apparent suicides, both found with cryptic messages."

"More tip-offs then? I'm wondering where you're getting all this from, John. We don't have leaky pipes here. The super made sure we tightened up on that recently."

She doesn't sound too pleased, but I'm used to this kind of awkward chat with the police.

"Are you planning to run this, John? It's very early days in both investigations."

I realise I am planning to run it, assuming the editor bites. I tell Morrison I'll keep her informed on publication as a courtesy and avoid speculation on whether they were suicides or otherwise.

More digging reveals Jeremy Grover was the finance director at AD&D Timber. So, both men worked in raw materials and both were found with reports about unscrupulous activities in those industries in South

America.

I keep my news report short and emphasise that police are appealing for information on two mysterious deaths that may be connected. I'm done in twenty minutes. It's a relief to know I've still got it. I message Steve to tell the news desk I'll be filing my first article in months.

Steve calls me straight away. "Hey, mate. That's great you're filing a story. I thought it would do you good to get back to it. Have you any idea who sent that USB then?"

I haven't told Steve anything about the phone calls yet. I definitely don't want him to know about the first call on Beachy Head, that's for sure.

"A man called me after I opened those files. He said he was a private investigator."

"Hmm. Well, your number's on file at the paper. Maybe he sweet-talked someone."

"Probably."

"Listen, John. We're worried about you. I've been talking to a friend of Alison's and she said it would do you good to talk things through after such a trauma. She helps a lot of people."

"Are you talking about therapy, Steve? I don't know about that. Not my thing."

"Maybe it is, maybe it isn't, but at least think about it, John. It might help."

I know Steve means well but I don't want some shrink poking around my brain. I don't think I'd like what she'd find.

"Okay. I'll think about it."

I'm lying. I can't think of anything worse. I don't want to think about anything right now. Just doing that bit of work has left me exhausted and my head hurts. I lie back on the pillow and try to drift away.

Chapter 7

I remember my phone ringing that afternoon. I didn't recognise the number so I let it go to voicemail. I needed to get on with my report, otherwise I'd miss the deadline.

It was an hour later when I checked voicemail. "This is a message for John Adamson. It's Gregorio Morales from the British embassy in Quito. Please call me back when you receive this message – it's urgent."

Why the hell didn't I answer the phone? I phoned back and Morales asked me to confirm Christina Bautista as my wife. "Mr Adamson, I'm afraid your wife has been taken very ill. She is in intensive care in Quito. The hospital informs me it is suspected dengue fever."

I remember jumping back from the phone like I'd received an electric shock. He gave me the address of the hospital and that was the end of the conversation.

I only knew vaguely what dengue fever was. You were hardly ever ill. I told myself you were young and strong. You'd be okay.

I don't know what they use to torture people but it could be waiting on a customer service call, listening to electronic muzak, trying desperately to book a flight to race across the world. I gave up waiting and drove straight to Heathrow instead.

First class was all they had but I couldn't wait until the next day. I'd never flown first class before. It was nauseating when the stewardess kept asking me if I wanted this or that. No, I don't want complimentary champagne – what on earth was there to celebrate? I told her to leave me alone.

It was a night flight. I was surrounded by men in suits, tucking into their gourmet meals and quaffing wine, but at least I had my own space and they weren't too close to me. The seat turned into a bed. Ironic that it was the best seat I'd ever had on a flight and I couldn't sleep a wink. Torture isn't a customer service queue after all; it's sitting in a cabin counting down fourteen hours, staring at a map of the world, willing the plane to move faster.

It was six a.m. when we touched down in Quito. I'm usually one of those people that waits until everyone else has rushed off the plane, but I couldn't get off fast enough. No luggage to collect at least – I had no time to pack.

I hailed a taxi outside the airport. The driver's eyes lit up at the sight of a *gringo*. Twenty dollars for a few miles? Usually, I'd argue or stomp off to look for another cab, but there was no time for my outraged foreigner routine. Please just drive fast like a lunatic, that's it. Hold on, Christina, I'm coming.

The clinic looked modern. That gave me hope that the doctors knew what they were doing. I asked the receptionist for intensive care and followed the signs up the stairs along the corridor. Another reception. I gave them your name and the receptionist looked at me with what looked like pity. A shiver came over me. She told me to wait. Anything but more waiting!

A grey-haired doctor came through, shook my hand and told me in broken English: "I'm sorry, Señor Adamson, but your wife Christina died an hour ago. Multiple organ failure. I am very sorry for your loss."

I couldn't breathe. I backed against the wall and slid down to the floor.

I don't remember much else until I was led into a room. I must have asked to see you. As the nurse lifted the sheet, I still hoped they had the wrong person. I'd never wanted so desperately *not* to see your face, but it was your face. You could have been sleeping. Eyes closed; mouth slightly open. Your skin was so pale.

I brought my hand to your cheek. It was still warm. I kissed your forehead and rested my head on your abdomen, the place where I hoped you would bear our children. Our future gone.

I must have lay there for a long time until I became aware of a soft tap at the door. The nurse entered, looking awkward as she asked me to come with her. "*Papeles*," she said. She wanted me to deal with some paperwork.

I went back to reception where a tall man in a cream suit was gesticulating angrily at a doctor and pointing at a sheet of paper. He saw me and straightened up.

"Mr Adamson, I'm so sorry for your loss. It must be a terrible shock."

He appeared to be waiting for a response. I whispered thanks.

"I'm Charles Campbell. I work um... with the embassy on an ad hoc basis. I'm here to help you in any way I can."

I nodded and he continued. "I'm so sorry to have to do this but we need to sort out some paperwork. Here is the death certificate." He said this in a hushed tone, hesitating before handing me the document.

There it was in black and white: Christina Bautista, aged 33. My eyes scanned down to the cause of death: 'dengue.'

I asked, "Are they sure it was dengue fever?" My voice was hoarse. I could scarcely get the words out.

"I'm afraid so. They tested for it. Apparently, she was staying in such a remote location in the jungle that it took time to get her to a decent hospital. If it turns cerebral, it's very dangerous. I'm so sorry."

Campbell picked up more papers and drew a sharp intake of breath. He started talking about insurance and payment. I wasn't listening. His words were like a radio going in and out of frequency. "Bill needs to be settled... claim back later... two days' intensive care...

words with the manager… come to an agreement."

"An agreement?" I looked him in the eye for the first time.

Campbell blushed and lowered his voice. "In this country, often with foreigners, prices suddenly go up. I did what I could, you see."

Campbell handed me a bill for $3,425. I hadn't got the energy to argue and, as he said, I could claim it back on insurance. I didn't want to talk about something as petty as money anyway. I didn't want to talk at all.

"We also need to cover the arrangements because the hospital will charge you more if the body is kept here another night. Now, I understand Christina had dual nationality but you were residing in the UK. The difficulty is that repatriation of a body is, well, complicated and expensive."

He paused, then added, "If I might make a suggestion?"

I spread my hands in exasperation. There didn't seem much point in doing anything other than give the appearance of listening.

"A cremation here might be your best option. Then you can have a proper memorial in England. That or… burial here."

I finally found my voice. "Mr Campbell, thank you for your help but I need to spend some time with my wife, then I will deal with this."

"Of course, old chap. I don't want to intrude. Merely here to help. Organising these things can be a nightmare, so here's my card. I'll be in the office for the rest of the day."

I was relieved to see him go. I needed to be with you, one last time.

***

Part of me wishes I could erase those few days from my mind, but the memory is burnt into my brain like a branding iron.

I have so little control over the triggers that take me back there – a plane flying over the city, a phone call from an unrecognised number, the buzz of a mosquito. On this occasion, it was reading Christina's blog.

As I lie on the bed staring at the ceiling, reliving every excruciating memory, a new thought has entered my mind: I shouldn't have agreed to a cremation so quickly. Why did I do that?

I was shell-shocked, traumatised, and Charles Campbell had a point. The idea of drawing out my agony by trying to repatriate Christina's body… no. I definitely didn't want her buried five thousand miles away either.

They performed an autopsy the same day, confirming the original diagnosis. But after what Root said on the phone, and those comments on the blog, maybe it wasn't dengue fever at all. How can I ever know the truth though when another autopsy is now impossible? All that's left of Christina are ashes in an urn. I haven't scattered them yet; I can't face doing that.

I'm under no illusions about how difficult this will be, but the comments on the blog really woke me up and jolted me out of my alcohol stupor. It could be the hardest investigation I will ever do but I can't ignore what is staring me in the face.

I've looked into dengue fever and the numbers really don't add up. Less than five per cent of cases develop into the more dangerous haemorrhagic type that affects the brain, and under five per cent of these cases are fatal. So, either Christina was incredibly unlucky, or it simply wasn't dengue. The diagnosis could have been wrong, but now I'm wondering if someone deliberately fabricated it.

I need to start with that diagnosis – the doctors in Ecuador, Charles Campbell and the embassy. I look in my wallet and I still have his card: 'Charles Campbell, Business Consultant, British Embassy, Quito.' It seems an odd title.

I try the phone number but it goes straight to an automated voicemail in Spanish. I look up the embassy number and call, asking for Gregorio Morales, the man who phoned originally to tell me Christina was in hospital.

He remembers me clearly. "Good morning, Mr Adamson. I was so sorry to hear of your loss. How can I be of assistance?"

"Thank you. I'm trying to get hold of Charles Campbell, who helped me in Ecuador. Could you put me through please?"

"I'm sorry, Mr Adamson, but Mr Campbell does not work directly for the embassy. He is a consultant. He works mainly with the Chamber of Commerce. Are you calling from the UK? Because I believe he is in London at present. He spends a lot of time there."

"Do you have a contact number for him?"

"I'm sorry, no. I will ask colleagues and let you know if I can locate it."

He's easier to find if he's in London. It doesn't take me long searching online at Companies House. There is a Campbell and Associates Consulting registered in Belgravia. It could be him.

I call and a rather haughty secretary confirms it is the office of Charles Campbell, but he is in meetings all day. At least I've located him. I ask to make an appointment, but after being put on hold, she tells me he's fully booked all week.

Patience is not a virtue of mine. I don't take no for an answer when I'm looking for information and I will never change. It annoys people sometimes, but I get what I want more quickly.

Belgravia is right next to Victoria so it's only a fifteen-minute train ride away. I decide to follow my journalistic instinct and go there this afternoon.

It feels strange to leave the flat. This is the first time I've been outside since that night on Beachy Head. I squint at the sun as I walk to the station. South London is going about its business as always. The city hasn't changed, but I have. I catch sight of myself in a shop window. I need to shave and comb my unruly hair. At least I put on a jacket and shirt, but I look more haggard than respectable.

The Belgravia office is impressive – a five-storey townhouse with an archway and bay windows. There are several companies listed with a shared reception area. It's just before five p.m. so I shouldn't have long to wait until Campbell is done for the day.

It's the same receptionist that answered the phone. I give her my best 'screw you' smile and assure her it's fine for me to wait without an appointment. She makes a fuss, but I ignore it and take a seat.

It's not long before I hear a booming voice, and a tall man in a navy blue suit emerges from the staircase. It's Charles Campbell talking with two other businessmen. "So good of you to come on such short notice. I'll get my team to prepare the paperwork and have it sent over to you."

I wait until he's seen them off before I stand up and call out to him. "Mr Campbell?"

He turns, frowning, and sees me. His eyes widen.

"Good Lord. Mr… um…"

I complete his sentence. "Adamson. I'm sorry for the intrusion but I wondered if I might have a few moments of your time? I did call ahead but your assistant said your schedule was very full. I have a few questions about my wife and what happened in Ecuador."

"Terrible thing what happened to your wife…" He

seems to be trying to remember her name.

"Christina."

"Yes, of course. You have questions, you say? Have you directed them to the embassy? I'm not sure what further help I can be at this point. Can I ask what sort of questions?"

"I'd rather discuss in private if possible. Do you have time now? I'm sure it wouldn't take long."

"This is a little irregular, but of course I will do what I can. I'm afraid I have to dash now though."

Campbell starts fumbling in his jacket pocket and consults a diary.

"I've had to revert to the old diary as we had an email crash the other week. I lost my phone as well. Disastrous. Lost a lot of information. Most inconvenient."

He leafs through the diary. "I could see you in the morning before my first appointment. Eight thirty?"

"Perfect, see you then."

Charles Campbell doesn't look very happy about it.

Chapter 8

I need to start at the beginning in this investigation, which means not only interviewing Campbell and contacting the hospital, but understanding as much as possible about what Christina was doing in Ecuador, and the scope of her research.

Root told me to read the blog more closely, so I'm going through it methodically. I go back to her first post from six months ago.

Back to my roots

I have treasured memories of the forest, maybe that's why I feel constantly drawn back to it. I love sitting under the trees and never feel alone among such wise, old souls.

When I was a girl, I used to visit my father in Spain on vacations. He had a cottage on the edge of a forest on the slopes of the Pyrenees. I would steal away for long afternoons in the woodland, exploring wilder areas away from the hiking trails. I'd enjoy the adventure of clambering through foliage and endure the sting of thorns scraping my legs. It felt fitting to give the forest a little of my blood. Papi would fuss over me later when I got back and he would dab my knees with antiseptic. Even now the smell of it makes me think of him and smile.

The scratches were worth it though because my reward would be my secret place. It took me a while to find but I would spend hours there in a hollow surrounded by beech and fir trees. It was far away from people, just the way I liked it.

The hollow was mine, I liked to think, but I knew deep down that it belonged to the forest and I was merely a guest of the trees that guarded it. I even named them: Theodore, Frederick, Isabel, Elizabeth. It's funny to think of that now. How pretentious I could be! I gave them grand names as if they were monarchs and greeted them with a reverential nod before sitting cross-legged and letting my imagination take me where it wanted. I would close my eyes with the sun warming my face and fly over a forest that stretched endlessly to the horizons of my imagination.

My love of the forest has now drawn me back to my country. El bosque nublado, la selva – these were places I never visited as a child growing up on the coast. Mami used to tell me the jungle was a wild place filled with creatures that could kill us. I wonder now if her attitude was partly an attempt to forget where she came from. Like most Ecuadorians, she was mixed race with some indigenous blood, but while the word 'mestiza' may be used in books, I've never heard anyone of mixed race use that word in Ecuador. Switch on the TV and you'd think Ecuador was a white country – white skin, botox and plastic noses! And the antiquated obsession with the family name drives me crazy. Many trace their roots back to the Spanish conquistadors, as if it was something to be proud of. So your family's ancestors were rapists and murderers who stole tribal land? How impressive!

Maybe one of the reasons I never felt truly at home in Ecuador was the obsession with ethnicity and skin colour. My mother was darker skinned – 'canela', like cinnamon sugar she used to say while stroking her face. I could tell she wished she was whiter though, due to the stigma. She was delighted that I had lighter skin like my dad, which pained me a bit because I always thought she was so beautiful. I found it ironic when I came to England to find so many women were obsessed with looking tanned – it seems women all over the world want to look different to how they were born to impress society and be happy!

I could do an entire project on race in Ecuador, but I'm more interested in how our species cares for – and neglects – other species. Ecuador is so diverse, it's incredible. I remember the first time I drove all the way from the coast through the Andes to the edge of the jungle in about nine hours – no more than going from London to Edinburgh. It was like experiencing three completely different countries in the same day!

There are many great projects in Ecuador that protect the biodiversity, and these are needed more than ever with the pressure ever greater to exploit land for oil, minerals and farming. My hope is that I can find examples of best practice in my country and spread the word about them to encourage more investment and more visitors. It's going to be an exciting trip!

Christina's optimism was just one of the qualities I adored about her. She was full of enthusiasm for her project, like everything she did.

It's poignant to hear her writing so fondly about her father. I remember she had a troubled relationship with him and was devastated when he died of a sudden heart attack. Reading these words though, I wonder how long it would take for me to start talking about Christina with the same warm feelings of nostalgia as she talked about her dad. Could I ever do that? At least her father made it to sixty-one. Not very old, but not a bad innings. Christina was so young and had so much more life in her.

I don't have time to fall into another pit of sadness today. It's time to leave. I'm hoping to get some more insight from Charles Campbell into what happened in Ecuador.

I head into the city on a packed commuter train. It's been quite a while since I've done this. It strikes me how so many people can be so close to each other and yet disconnected, so alone. Unreal city.

I pick up a copy of *The Sentinel* outside the station. I've always liked the printed page more than the internet because I grew up reading it. My first article in months is on page ten – quite short and not particularly prominent but I wasn't expecting it to be. The headline is: *Police appeal on mysterious deaths*. They haven't edited it down much – there are the details on Blakely and Grover, and the fact they were missing for several days. I emphasised the police were so far treating the deaths as 'unexplained' and appealing for information on the men's whereabouts in the days before their deaths. I included a quote from DCI Morrison to that effect. At her request, I didn't mention the words 'oil' and 'timber' were found at the scene. I may do so in any follow-up though.

I reach Campbell's office just after eight a.m. The receptionist is there already and confirms my appointment in a cold, business-like manner. I smile and apologise for yesterday's 'intrusion' and stress the urgency of my meeting. I've learnt over the years that receptionists, secretaries, personal assistants – whatever title they assume – are often the biggest hurdle to speaking to those in positions of power. I've made a habit of bypassing them but also charming them when necessary. It's not working this time though. She looks at me like I'm something she cleaned off her shoe.

After ten minutes, the phone rings and she tells me to go up to the third floor office. Charles Campbell greets me outside the lift and breaks into a smile. It looks forced. He gives me a brief look up and down. He is suited up, while my jacket and unironed shirt look informal in comparison. Dressing to impress has never been my style.

Campbell is taller than I remember, and older too – a full head of hair but grey. His handshake is angled downwards and firm. He probably wants to let me know who is in charge.

"How are you, my dear chap? You've really been through the mill."

"Not great, but a little better than I was."

He indicates for me to take a seat.

"Take it day by day, that's all you can do. Now, before we start, I'm aware you are a journalist so I just wanted to clarify this is a private chat. I presume you are not here in any… um… professional capacity?"

"Of course not, Mr Campbell. I did my best to keep any coverage of my wife's death out of the media at the time – thank you for your help on that too. This is not for publication. I simply need to get a few things clear for my own peace of mind."

He seems satisfied. "Call me Charles, please."

"I understand you met Christina. She said you were quite helpful at the beginning of her trip."

Campbell frowns, stroking his chin. "Well, I met her briefly. She told me a little of her research. I gave her a few pointers on some areas further south that may have been of interest. I know Ecuador well, you see, having done business there for many years."

I used an old trick there, pretending to know more than I do. I didn't actually know if he'd met Christina.

"Did she follow your advice and go to those areas?"

"I have no idea. I do know she was upstream from Lago Agrio when she became ill. It's not the best of areas in the *Oriente* – that's what they call the Amazon area in Ecuador – although I can't think of a place more different to the Orient."

"Not the best area. How so?"

"The Colombian border, the remnants of FARC rebel groups, drug trafficking, that sort of thing. I actually told Christina it was an area to avoid, but…" He spread his hands wide to indicate that she didn't listen. I feel immediately irritated by that.

"Do you know if dengue fever outbreaks are common there? From my research, it seems uncommon."

"Hard to say. She was terribly unlucky, but dengue outbreaks happen in many areas of Ecuador. Malaria far less so. I had a good friend who died in East Africa from that disease so I know something of what you've been through. But losing your wife – I can't imagine how hard that would be."

"Thank you, and thank you for being so helpful at the hospital. I need to clear something up though. I thought you worked at the embassy and in fact I think you told me that, but the embassy says that's not the case. What do you do for work exactly?"

48

"Officially, I work with the Chamber of Commerce and do consultancy, mainly on agricultural exports. As you probably know, most of Ecuador's economy is raw materials."

"Right, so not directly with the embassy. So, forgive me, but how is it you came to be at the hospital that day then, if it wasn't in your remit? I'm just trying to understand."

"Oh, well, my brother-in-law is a doctor at that hospital as it happens. A paediatrician though, so he didn't treat your wife, but he informed me a British citizen had arrived in a critical condition."

"And did you speak directly to the doctor who tested for dengue?"

"Erm no, but it's a good hospital. I would say close to Western standards actually. I had no reason to doubt it."

"But the odds of dengue turning so bad so quickly are quite slim, if my research is right, so I'm wondering if the diagnosis was correct."

"Oh, but there was an autopsy that confirmed it, correct?"

"Correct."

"Mr Adamson, can I ask: is there anything that has prompted these doubts?"

I've already decided to keep my cards close to my chest, and I'm not going to tell him about any anonymous tip-offs, that's for sure.

"It just doesn't really add up."

49

He considers it for a moment. "A death in the family is a huge shock. I think it's perfectly normal to look for answers, but you could be torturing yourself to no avail, old chap."

"I need to be sure. I'm sure you can understand that. I think I should try to contact the community where she was staying in Ecuador."

Campbell frowns. "Perhaps. A word of caution though. My experience of Ecuador is that rumours fly around, especially when it comes to the... um... primitive peoples that live there. They don't actually believe in natural death, you know. To them, any disease is the result of an enemy medicine man conjuring invisible darts and suchlike."

He breaks into an exasperated smile, shaking his head. There's something I dislike about the way he wrinkled his nose at the word 'primitive'.

"Anyway, I do have a client arriving soon so I have to wrap this up. Here's my email address though if you want to contact me again, but I think I've told you all I can."

He gets up and extends his hand. Our eyes meet briefly and he looks away. I turn and leave.

Chapter 9

I remember that day vividly. It was one of those ethereal mornings in the Andes when the sky was deep blue and the faint morning chill gave way to the sun streaming through crisp mountain air.

At nearly two thousand metres above sea level, I thought the cool climate of Baños was heavenly. There was none of the biting cold of the higher plains, nor the often oppressive heat of the lowlands.

An early morning thermal bath in the open air sounded irresistible, but I didn't know it would change my life. I was on sabbatical from the media madness and had decided to linger in Baños a few days longer than originally intended because I loved the place. The town was in foothills below the active volcano Tungurahua, which I'd read translated as 'Throat of Fire' in the indigenous language Kichwa. Even though Baños was only a few miles from the volcano, the town lay on the opposite side to the crater, so I was safe apparently.

I wasn't alone in thinking it the perfect day for a dip. The locals were up early too and the baths, *Piscinas de la Virgen*, swelled with the chatter and laughter of families. I felt self-conscious. Surrounded by tanned bodies, I looked glaringly pallid. A couple of teenage girls giggled as I walked past them. I'd been in Ecuador a few weeks and still couldn't tell whether these regular fits of giggles from local girls were in appreciation or ridicule. Maybe a bit of both. I just smiled back.

I made for the hottest of the three baths – forty-five degrees, according to the sign on the wall. At first glance, the water didn't appear enticing at all. "It looks like a steaming cloudy yellow pool of piss," one backpacker had told me when I arrived. He was kidding – at least about the bath's contents I hoped – but the description of their appearance was spot on. I reminded myself these were sulphurous volcanic baths, rich in minerals and renowned for healing properties. After a few crazy months at work, I needed some healing.

I was about to get in when a voice called out: "What about your watch?" I looked up to see a young woman with long, brown wavy hair, dangling her legs in the water playfully. She cocked her head to one side at me with an enquiring smile.

I looked at my wrist, then shrugged: "It's waterproof."

I blushed. It wasn't a good answer.

She sighed dramatically. "Ah, but is it hot volcanic bath-proof?"

She had me there. I did a comical double-take. I was overacting, showing off a bit. She threw her head back and laughed. I remember watching her as she did so. It was a beautiful sight and a beautiful sound.

I took my watch back to my locker and returned to the hot bath with a spring in my step. We chatted some more before moving to the larger middle bath, which was a more comfortably warm temperature for a longer soak.

I was surprised to hear that Christina was from Ecuador, given her fluent English and lack of accent, although I could detect a trace of American twang. She told me her father was Spanish and she'd been educated in an international high school.

She seemed fascinated to hear about my media career. "So you've actually helped catch bad guys? That's great. They rarely catch them here as their *amigos* run the justice system."

Christina insisted we plunge into the cold pool. "It wakes you up ready for the day, otherwise you'll feel sleepy." I protested that I was on holiday so a siesta sounded good, but I wasn't going to wimp out. I'd already decided this woman was worth impressing.

She was right; I felt fantastic after a spell in the cold pool. Later, we stood next to each other in the outdoor showers as she washed her hair. I don't know what possessed me but I reached out and continued lathering her hair, running my fingers through the thick strands. She opened her eyes and smiled at me. "That's new," she said, before adding, *"atrevido,"* and pouting playfully. I looked up that word later. It meant 'cheeky'.

I felt a knot in my stomach. I remember looking around at the valley and back at the beautiful woman next to me, thinking that I wouldn't mind staying here with her forever.

I open my eyes. Jessica is listening to my story intently. When it's clear I've finished for now, she smiles and nods. "Thanks for sharing, John. Sounds like it was a magical day."

Jessica is a friend of Steve's wife Alison. Steve cajoled me into coming to a therapy session and told me he'd already paid for it. This isn't how I expected the session to go though. After a few information-gathering questions, Dr Bainbridge, who insisted I call her Jessica, asked me to tell her about when I first met Christina. I haven't reminisced about that day for a very long time.

"So how does it feel to remember and talk about it now?"

Oh, here we go. It was all going so well, but now I have to talk about my feelings. I can't just reminisce.

"It felt nice to go back to that day, but it's sad to remember now when so much has changed."

"Of course. A few months is not long at all and memories can be painful, but it was a happy day and it's important to try to remember that. Good memories can be a comfort too."

"The problem is that remembering is all I do. And what were good memories now feel even worse. Just when there's a chink of light in a day, I see something of Christina's or I remember something, then I feel hopeless. *She* was the light."

I talk more about Christina's belongings, which are still all over the flat. I say that putting them away would feel too much like trying to forget her. Jessica suggests creating a space to put things so that I can take them out and look at them when I choose rather than reacting to constant triggers. It makes sense and maybe it works for some people, but it feels insensitive to start packing her things into a box.

As much as it helps to say these things out loud rather than leave thoughts stewing in my head, I'm relieved when Jessica brings the session to a close. I don't think therapy is for me. It's exhausting. I doubt I'll go back any time soon.

Coming out of the office, Kensington High Street is bursting with tourists as usual, no doubt going to the museums. I head back into the city to a café in Farringdon to meet Steve.

After thinking it through, I decided to tell Steve about the phone call from Root and my suspicions about what happened to Christina. I put it all in an email, but didn't mention the text message on Beachy Head. Some things are best kept under wraps, and I don't want Steve worrying even more about me.

Steve is already sat down, chatting to an attractive waitress. She's laughing and playing with her hair. How does he do it? He may be in his late thirties, but he looks ten years younger. When he grew a thick blond moustache for Movember a couple of years ago, he looked like a young Robert Redford. He even got stopped at the airport by tourists. I could be invisible next to Steve where women are concerned. I used to joke with Christina that I was glad he didn't come with me on my sabbatical to Ecuador, otherwise I wouldn't have had a chance with her. She told me not to be so silly.

He may attract attention but Steve adores his wife Alison, and their two blond boys are the spitting image of him. I used to look at their family and hope it would be a glimpse of our own future. I don't begrudge him happiness though. He deserves it.

"Alright, Sundance?" I call out.

"Hey, Butch." Steve flashes me a grin.

The waitress takes my order and leaves us to it.

"I've got some news for you, mate. Rupert threw his toys out of the pram. I think he was hoping you wouldn't be back for a while. He up and left to work for some right-wing start-up."

"Really? That's a shame." I can't hide a wry smile. Rupert has shown his true colours then. He never struck me as a *Sentinel* reader.

"Yeah, go figure. So how was the session with Jessica?"

"It started off okay, reminiscing about memories, but once we got into talking about feelings, it was exhausting."

"I hear you, mate, but you know, it might help in the long term even if it's hard at first."

"Maybe."

Steve knows me well enough to realise I'm humouring him and changes the subject. "We definitely need to talk about what you told me over email. I mean, it's bad enough losing Christina but now you've got this stranger planting ideas in your head."

"Not just planting ideas, Steve. I told you about the blog posts and the comments."

"Yes, but it's not much to go on so far, is it? Have you considered this guy might be leading you on a wild goose chase to get you to cover this story, for whatever reason?"

"Yes, I've considered that possibility, but what choice have I got? It's in my head now. I can't ignore it. I need to find out for sure if something else happened to Christina."

"Okay, true. For the sake of argument, let's say he's onto something. Then basically the hospital in Ecuador must have either got it wrong or deliberately falsified a diagnosis and an autopsy."

"That's possible in Ecuador with the right connections."

"Possible then, but short of going out there and trying to find the doctors – who would deny it anyway – how would we know for sure?"

I'm glad to hear Steve say 'we'. This is not something I want to tackle alone and he's a tenacious investigative reporter.

"Did you get much from this British guy?"

"Campbell. He was at the hospital. Not much. I don't know, he was a bit cagey."

"How do you mean?"

I sigh and shrug. All I have is hunches and hearsay. It puts into perspective the task I face to piece it all together. I have so little to go on, but it's a relief to share it with Steve.

We chat a little more, then I get the train back to Croydon. My neighbourhood is a bit rough around the edges, but we bought so far out of the city to get extra space. I could only have afforded a hole in the wall in the centre. Telling people in the media I lived in Croydon was a sure-fire way to discover the pretentious idiots. Rupert actually said, "You have my sympathies." That made it easier to despise him.

I have a love–hate relationship with London. Tired of London, tired of life they say. I am definitely tired and not sleeping much, but I have something to get up for now – motivation to find out what happened to Christina.

Steve is right though. What do I have so far? Possible threats on Christina's blog over her investigations. Suspicions about the hospital but no evidence. Campbell mentioned *guerrillas* and Lago Agrio not being the best of areas, but I doubt that's relevant. If FARC or some similar group had been involved, it would have been obvious and unlikely they would have covered it up. I still wonder why Campbell was at the hospital though if it wasn't really his remit. He also seemed to be trying to dissuade me from investigating further.

I get home and open my computer. There's a new email, this time from the address 'rootandbranch001'. He does like his word play and seems to have an endless list of email accounts.

Dear John,

Good you're writing again but you can do better than that report, come on!

Maybe you need a bit more motivation. I attach something that might do the trick.

I expect more detail next time. Quid pro quo.

R

His teasing is getting annoying, and he's criticising my writing now. I open up the attachment. It's a screenshot. I enlarge it to view some kind of data file. At the top is Christina's blog address. There are various numbers and some rows are highlighted: *Published: 42MB. Unpublished: 14MB.*

I don't know how he got this information. Maybe he has hacking skills. It must be held on the blog server or inside the actual blog, but the meaning is clear – there is content on Christina's blog that isn't published, that I haven't seen.

I need to find a way to get inside the blog account to read it.

Chapter 10: Liu

Dear Mr Liu,

We are looking forward to seeing you at our exclusive preview of London's new gourmet Brazilian steak restaurant, Churrascaría.

Please be advised that due to unforeseen circumstances, the venue has been changed to 36b Romilly Street, London at seven p.m.

Please also note that due to limited numbers, we cannot accommodate a plus one on this occasion. We apologies for any inconvenience.

You will be met by our restaurant manager Ricardo Silva, and our chef Fidel will prepare for you what has been described by one prominent food critic as 'the finest steak on the planet'.

We look forward to cooking you a delicious meal and discussing some exciting opportunities to do business together in the future.

Liu re-read the email to check the address. He was looking forward to this. It was something he loved about

London. There was always somewhere new to eat and 'the finest steak on the planet' – that was quite a claim and impossible to resist. It would be something to tell his friends back in China if true.

His family was very proud he had secured such a good position in the food industry, and he was proud to serve his country by providing the finest quality meat. He loved steak in particular. People were meant to be carnivores, and he couldn't imagine life without meat. Vegetarians and animal rights people annoyed him, and there were a lot of them in London. He didn't understand it. Animals were on the planet for the benefit of human beings.

It was a shame he couldn't bring a partner to the restaurant though. There was a lady in sales he'd been hoping to impress, but no matter. He had a few more evenings here so there would be more opportunities. Business was very good at present, so perhaps he could wow her at one of the more exclusive places.

He walked from Leicester Square underground station, ignoring a protester who tried to hand him a flyer, and took a minor detour along Gerrard Street to admire London's Chinatown.

He arrived on Romilly Street and checked the address again. Strange. There wasn't a restaurant at number 36, nor a buzzer for 36b. He took out his new phone, which replaced the one he'd lost the week before. He wondered if he'd been pickpocketed. It was very common in London, but the replacement had arrived fast, much to his relief. He had his entire life on his phone.

Just as he was looking at the phone map with puzzlement, the door opened and an attractive young blonde woman smiled at him. "Mr Liu? I'm so sorry for the last-minute change. I'm afraid the decorators let us down and the main dining area isn't ready yet, but we've prepared something special for you. Let me show you in."

Liu hesitated for a moment before following her upstairs. This didn't look like a restaurant. On the second floor, she opened a door to a dimly lit room. There was a small round table set for two at the centre of the room. Liu looked around to see it was otherwise completely empty; there were no other tables.

"I am the only person invited? I thought there would be other guests."

"Oh, there are other guests of course, but we wanted to offer a personalised service. There were guests at lunch and we have more coming after you. But please don't worry. We want to you to take your time to enjoy the experience."

She flashed him a smile and pulled back a chair, inviting him to sit.

"Can I interest you in a glass of Brazilian Merlot? It's lesser known than Chilean or Argentinian, but I think you'll find it's of excellent quality." She filled his glass.

"And can I check that your steak cooked medium rare is acceptable? It's the chef's recommendation."

Liu thought about it before nodding.

"I am just going to check on the manager's arrival. He will accompany you at dinner. The food is nearly ready."

She disappeared through a door at the back of the room. The faint smell of frying meat wafted through. Liu sipped his wine and smiled to himself. He deserved these kinds of treats. He worked very hard to bring the finest South American steak to top restaurants in Chinese cities, and sampling it was one of the perks. Business and pleasure.

A tall, broad-shouldered man with glasses and dark hair came through a few minutes later, carrying a plate of food. He was dressed in a tailored dark grey suit. Liu noticed with approval that his tie was decorated with green dragons. Clearly not a waiter.

"Mr Liu. Thank you so much for coming. I am the manager, Ricardo Silva." He extended his hand and shook a little too firmly for Liu's liking.

He gestured around the room. "I must apologise for the change of venue. As you can see, this is not our intended dining area, but I can assure you the food and wine are as intended."

With a flourish, he set down a plate of thinly cut steak, sautéed potatoes and asparagus. Liu took his time cutting a slice of steak and put it in his mouth. Tender with a hint of garlic. It was acceptable, but hardly the finest he'd tasted. He frowned at a slightly bitter aftertaste.

"How do you like the steak, Mr Liu?"

"It is… good." It was important to put on his best face. After all, he'd been shown hospitality and the restaurant owners had made clear in communications of their ambition to do more business in Asia. There could be opportunities to make money here.

Liu continued eating but began to feel uncomfortable that the manager was watching him silently and smiling. Suddenly, Mr Silva turned and produced a remote control. To Liu's surprise, an electronic screen flickered on in the corner opposite him.

"I have prepared a short presentation. I hope you don't object. I thought you'd like to see where the beef comes from."

The screen showed an aerial shot of grasslands and cattle. The orchestral background music was dramatic as the camera panned past the grasslands towards a forest.

The camera moved deeper over the forest before cutting to a new shot at ground level. The forest was dense, the trees swaying in the breeze. In the background, Liu could make out an orange glow.

The manager spoke. "The beef you are eating comes from cattle that graze on land that for thousands of years previously was rainforest. Did you know that, Mr Liu?"

Liu frowned. The manager didn't wait for him to answer.

"The quickest way to clear the forest is with fires. Did you know that forest fires can travel at three metres per second? Even faster across grasslands. It's impressive work your partners do, Mr Liu."

Liu choked briefly and swallowed a piece of steak before responding. "What do you mean *my partners*? I am in the food business. I don't start fires."

"Not personally, but you buy from people who do so to graze cattle so that you and your clients can eat steak."

The glow in the background had grown into flames climbing higher, catching one tree after another until the fire reached the branches of the largest tree in the centre of the screen.

Liu raised his voice. "This is not what I do. And I don't why you are showing me this video. I am uncomfortable, and I don't think you are someone I want to do business with. This steak is no more than adequate, not the 'finest on the planet'!"

Liu made to stand up but felt unsteady and sat down again. He loosened his tie and took a deep breath, shaking his head and blinking hard.

"But wait, Mr Liu. You have so much more to eat. We have another piece of steak for you when you finish that."

"I'm not hungry anymore." He slumped back into his chair.

"Oh, come now. I assure you the next piece you won't even swallow. It will melt in your mouth."

The manager's words reverberated in Liu's mind. He mumbled something as his head hit the plate, the flavour of beef in his nostrils as he lost consciousness.

Chapter 11

I've just finished breakfast when I receive an email entitled 'Third time lucky' from 'rootofallevil667'. The pun again. He never emails me from the same address twice – strangely evasive behaviour for a supposed private investigator.

The email contains only two words: 'Fresh meat', with a photo attached named '36b Romilly St'. I'm unprepared for what I see when I open it. A man at a table, his head tilted back. He looks Asian and is clearly dead. His mouth is wide open and full of something. I enlarge it. It looks like pieces of meat.

I feel nauseous. I can feel my breakfast in my throat. If there was any doubt about the first two deaths, there is none now. Nobody accidentally dies with his mouth crammed full of meat, the way this man did. First oil, then timber, now meat.

Time to murder and create.

I check the Met's website but there's nothing about a body found in central London. 36b Romilly Street – that's just off Chinatown.

He usually sends me the name of the victim, but this time he's sent me an exact address. Perhaps the body hasn't been found yet and he's telling me where to find it. That would be getting far more closely involved with this case than I'm comfortable with.

I deliberate over whether to phone DCI Morrison, but my journalistic instinct tells me to go there myself. If the police are already there, I can get an interview. If not, I want to see this crime scene.

I head into the city, take the underground to Leicester Square and cut through Chinatown to the address. It's a townhouse next to a café. I look on the buzzer but there is no 36b. That's weird. I try the door and to my surprise it's unlocked.

I can hear voices from an office on the ground floor. It can't be in there. I go up two flights of stairs and see an unmarked door. I push it and it's also unlocked.

This looks like the room from the photo – empty apart from a table and two chairs. The lights are on, illuminating the man in the centre of the room. It looks almost like a scene from a play with everything carefully arranged.

Standing alone in a room with a dead man is not something I'm used to. The victims are usually taken away by the time I arrive to report. The silence is what I notice first. Everything has stopped, but there's no serenity here, just a stale smell of cooking, which awakens my nausea again.

I approach the man at the table, treading lightly and

making sure I don't step on any evidence. Up close it's far worse than in the photos. His face is contorted, brownish pink slices of meat hanging from his mouth. His neck is taut, as rigor mortis has begun setting in. There's no decomposition though, so I don't think he's been here long.

The table has papers on it. There's a news report with the headline, 'Ranchers suspected of starting fires that wiped out Amazon tribe.' The word 'beef' is written across the middle of the report in a reddish-brown liquid that looks like a mix of blood and gravy. I take out my phone and photograph it.

Recalling what Morrison said about the first victim Blakely and his finger tracing the oil, I crouch by the victim to look at his hands hanging by his sides. There's a faint stain on the index. His finger traced the word then, probably guided by the killer when he was already dead.

There's a half-eaten plate of meat and vegetables on the table, the gravy congealed. In the centre of the table is an ash tray. There are seedlings lying in an inch or so of ash. "Out of their ashes, green shoots will grow," I murmur.

Suddenly I see a flash through the skylight. For a moment, I think I see someone out there on the roof. I can't be sure, but I have a strong feeling I shouldn't be here. I should call this in.

Just as I'm about to dial, I hear banging downstairs. Somebody's coming. I back out of the room and retreat up the next flight of stairs, just in time before several uniformed police officers rush into the room I've just left. They are quiet for a moment, no doubt surveying the grisly crime scene, then I hear them talking.

"Secure the scene, Sergeant." It's DCI Morrison on the radio.

This is not ideal. I knew I should have phoned Morrison. I can't hide here on the landing forever. Perhaps I can get away with pretending I arrived just after the police though. I walk quietly down the stairs. Luckily, the officers have their backs to the door. I stay outside and clear my throat. The sergeant spins around to see me already holding out a press card.

"Excuse me, officers. I got a tip-off about a crime here. Is DCI Morrison here?"

The sergeant is annoyed. "Christ, no press! How did you get here so fast? Wait outside, we haven't even secured the scene yet."

He ushers me out. I go downstairs and wait.

That was a close call, but perhaps worth the risk because this is a massive story. There's no doubt about it now. We've got a serial killer in London.

Chapter 12

Three men dead in spate of corporate killings

A man has been found murdered in central London, the third death in two weeks, sparking fears that a killer is targeting businessmen in the city.

That's the headline and lead of my first front-page exclusive for nearly a year. My article continues on page three, including the details of the messages and information left with the victims.

The other nationals are all playing catch-up and waiting for this morning's press conference at Scotland Yard. It's busy and most major media players are here. I see plenty of fellow hacks I've known for years. The mood is that odd mix of excitement and sombre determination from a pack of reporters on the scent of a murder enquiry.

Rupert Hennessy is here too, unfortunately, smoothing back his quiff like an overgrown private schoolboy, standing as close to the front as he can. I had a look at the start-up he's now writing for – *Free People News*. Seems to be yet another populist hard-right venture with money behind it – anti-immigration, low taxation, climate change denial, the usual stuff. We nod curtly at each other. At least we don't have to pretend to get along anymore.

Assistant Commissioner Stafford emerges from Scotland Yard. The police have clearly put the enquiry at a high level of priority if someone of his rank is speaking.

"Good morning, everyone. I will give a brief statement before taking questions. At nine thirty a.m. yesterday, police officers were called to an address on Romilly Street, London, where they found a deceased male identified as Chinese citizen Mr Gang Liu, aged 32. Initial pathology indicates he had been drugged and choked.

"There is sufficient evidence to link this death with two previously unexplained deaths of businessmen in the past month: Jeremy Grover, 38, found in an abandoned warehouse outside Guildford on 5th March, and Keith Blakely, 42, found dead in his car in Hampstead on 23rd February. The similarities both in forensics and in the messages left with the victims have led us to open a triple murder enquiry.

"We appeal to the public for any details of these men's movements in the days before their disappearance. Both Mr Grover and Mr Blakely were missing for several days before their bodies were discovered. We extend our sincere condolences to the families of these three men, who have had their lives cut short so tragically. I will take questions now."

Hennessy's hand shoots up and he launches straight in. "Can you give us further details of the messages left with the victims? Is it the case that the words 'oil', 'timber' and 'beef' were found with each victim, indicating the killer or killers may be targeting specific industries? Could they be politically motivated?"

Hennessy is over keen, asking too many questions at once. They are pertinent questions though, I'll grant him that.

Stafford frowns at him. "That's three questions, not one. I will not speculate on the motivation for the crimes at this point, but suffice to say the messages left at the scene give us reason to believe the crimes are connected."

I get a question in. "There were details of deaths in South America left with the victims. Could there be a connection and is it possible there is a vigilante element to these crimes?"

I know Stafford is far too cautious to be drawn on that, but it's worth a shot as it's my current theory. He responds. "I'm not going to comment further on possible motives, but we are investigating all the evidence from the scene. I want to add that I would urge the media not to speculate at this early stage of the enquiry."

He takes a couple more questions, confirming details

73

about the victims, last sightings and crime scenes, then brings the conference to a close. I try to get another question in but he's already walking away.

Stafford is wasting his breath appealing for journalists not to speculate. In my experience, before an arrest is made and charges brought, speculation is rife in the media. It's only when they catch someone that things tighten up because nobody wants to be held in contempt of court.

I don't hang around but head straight to the underground station. Just as I'm getting my ticket out, my phone buzzes. A text from an unknown number: "You ask the right questions, John. Good job. You're looking better too."

I feel my heart pounding. It's him. He must be watching me again. I look around, but I don't even know who I'm looking for. He must have been here somewhere at the press conference, and he wants me to know that. It's getting beyond creepy.

I hurry to get home. The story is all over the news with reporters already discussing possible motives. Although this case is enthralling, it's also a distraction from what is far more important to me. Root's 'quid pro quo' deal is getting frustrating. I'm sure he knows far more about Christina's death than he's let on, but he's feeding me scraps of information, one at a time.

The latest clue indicates there is unpublished content on Christina's blog, so I need to find a way to read it. I could try to do things officially and contact the blogging host with confirmation of her death and me as next of kin, but I couldn't guarantee they'd give me access and it would take a long time. It would be easier if I could just get into the blog myself. I have considered whether I should just ask Root directly to find a way in, as I presume he or someone he works with must have the IT skills to access that content log.

The problem with asking for his help is I'm becoming more convinced that Root is no private investigator. His access to photos of the crimes, not to mention his sick sense of humour, have led me to suspect he's involved somehow in these killings. To what extent I don't know, but it feels too uncomfortable to be getting information on my wife's death from someone who could be working with a murderer, or even doing the killings himself.

I need to try to get into this blog myself. I look through my emails and read several of Christina's messages. Her last email to me was sent in early October, the week before she died.

Hi darling,

Sorry again about the delay. I know I said I'd get to an internet connection more often, but it's been hard. Some things have happened here that I can't understand. I'll tell you about it all soon, so please don't worry.

I've been thinking about you a lot. I was thinking of the day we first met. The date and the place. I want us to go there again. I'll be thinking of that place all day today and this evening. If you do the same then we'll be thinking about the same thing at the same time! Then I can feel closer to you in that way, mi amor. Remember that day and that place, please. I'm glad I named my blog after it. I thought you'd like that!

I hope you can visit very soon. I'll put a date in the diary.

Love you to the stars and back,
Cx

This was the last communication I received from Christina. I've read it so often and cried over words I can recite by heart now. I'm reading it in a different light today though. It seemed very important to her that I thought of that day and that place, and she mentioned the blog.

There's something else: "I'll put a date in the diary." I hadn't noticed it before, but that phrase doesn't suit Christina at all. She would never say that to me. It's way too formal and business-like. I wonder now if she meant it literally and was trying to tell me something.

I go to the closet and take out her rucksack. It was returned to me at the hospital in Quito. I've looked through it many times – her sunglasses, washbag, camera, the scarf I bought her, some papers and an empty diary.

Christina didn't keep a diary as far as I knew so it's no surprise to me that it's empty. I wonder why it was in her bag though. I leaf through the diary carefully and stop at 5th April – my birthday. When I look closer, I realise it's not completely empty. There's faint scribble in pencil. I can just make out: 'pw (6) x.'

Of course. We often used our anniversary or each other's birthdays as passwords. Not very secure, granted, but this could be a stroke of luck. I don't know if this was a note for me to find, but I feel like Christina is here with me, giving me clues and willing me on.

I go to the blog site and try to log in. Six digits: 050482.

It works. I'm in.

Chapter 13

I'm excited. It's been months and I can't wait to see you. I've found out where you're staying in the jungle – an hour upstream from Lago Agrio. I pay a man at the docks to take a motorised canoe to the village.

I'm travelling deep into the jungle. As the boat slows down beside a mud bank, I can see you talking with some indigenous children. You turn around and your jaw drops in amazement, your hands cupped over your mouth. You break into that smile I adore. We run towards each other. It's like a climactic scene in a romantic movie. Tears are rolling down your cheeks.

I waste no time and whisk you off to an expensive lodge in the cloud forest, far from the Amazon. We make love all afternoon, wrapped in each other's arms. I've saved you. I've got you away from the jungle, away from disease and danger.

Sometimes I play this game in my mind, this flight of fancy. I think of what point in the past I would return to if I could go back in time to stop all this from happening. To change things, so I don't lose you.

I wonder when would be the best moment to return, going through various times as far back as before you left England. Could I go back and stop you from going to Ecuador? No, you would have resented that. We'd have argued and you'd probably have gone anyway.

I usually settle on this spur of the moment trip to visit you in the rainforest. I fly over to Ecuador and surprise you, take you out of the jungle. We take a vacation together and then I bring you home safely.

I allow myself to play out this fantasy and it comforts me for a short while, until I realise what I'm doing, then I'm snapped back to reality. I'm torturing myself. I have no time machine; I can't turn back the clock.

I don't want to face going to any more therapy sessions but I've started reading up on these feelings and the stages of grief. This one is called 'bargaining' apparently. The 'what ifs', the 'should haves'. Regrets and guilt – the idea that I could have done something. It's agonising and impossible to shake off.

Regrets are useless. If I spend my time ruing the past, I'm never going to be able to move forward. I know that, but some days I'm stuck in a cycle of self-flagellation, falling into a chasm between dreams and reality.

I need to find a way out of this. I need to know what happened in Ecuador, that much is clear. Perhaps it will give me a bit more peace of mind.

I may not know who Root is – and part of me doesn't want to know – but so far his leads have checked out. The blog contains far more than I realised. In the draft folder there are several unpublished posts. I read through the first one.

Yasuní: glimpses of heaven… and hell

Coca's name may not be as ugly as Lago Agrio, which translates as 'Sour Lake', but it's a troubled place. Coca has been the gateway to the jungle for years but now it's more of a hub for the oil industry. The colonial quest for gold has been replaced by a frenzied neo-colonial quest for black gold instead.

The town is dominated by a massive bridge across the river Napo. Rivers used to be the only way to travel but now roads are reaching ever further into the jungle. While I was waiting for a motorised canoe to go upriver, the waterfront felt unsafe with men hissing at me through their teeth. It's the kind of behaviour I hate most as a woman in this country. What kind of man hisses at a woman? My guide, Diego, was embarrassed and assured me the town was full of friendly people. He's a good man and keen to show me the reality of what's happening here.

It was a relief to leave Coca. Our canoe meandered up the river for over an hour before reaching a beach. We crossed to a smaller canoe and inched through flooded rainforest. Diego pointed out so many bird species on the way – tanagers, vultures, woodpeckers. Life was all around us.

When we arrived at the lodge, next to my cabin I saw

a pygmy marmoset in a tree. It's one of the smallest monkeys in the world. I adored the little guy!

In the afternoon, Diego took us to the top of a forty-five-metre observation tower, built around the sacred kapok tree. We saw parrots, toucans and a troupe of howler monkeys perched on the highest branch of the canopy, their roars echoing across the forest.

After a dinner of delicious fried maite – a river fish common in the area – we went on a night walk. I was totally out of my comfort zone! I'm not one of those squealy girls when it comes to creepy crawlies, but standing a couple of metres from a tarantula and then being told how far it can jump – eek! Diego reassured me they are mostly docile though and their bite is no worse than a wasp sting. He said he couldn't remember anyone ever getting bitten by one at the lodge either. I was still nervous though!

After the walk, we took a canoe ride through the dark waters. No anacondas thankfully, but we could make out the eyes of a white caiman watching us. It was exhilarating but I was also relieved to get back to the lodge.

The next day I finally entered a place I'd wanted to see for a long time – Yasuní National Park. The biodiversity there is amazing: twenty-five thousand species of plants and over sixteen hundred species of birds – more than the entire continent of North America.

The clay licks were the highlight. We waited in silence in an observation post for over an hour. One by one, birds appeared until dozens of cobalt-winged parakeets fluttered down and pecked at the water. After several minutes' drinking, without warning they flew straight at us through the lodge and back up into the trees. It was an incredible sight, but poignant too as I'm all too aware how threatened this region is. I wonder how long these birds will continue to drink here.

Diego told me the whole sorry story of Yasuní at dinner and it made me very angry. In 2007, the Ecuadorian government launched a plan to ask foreign governments to pay $3.6 billion to leave the oil in the ground under the national park. But by 2012, only $200 million had been raised. This is where it got scandalous. The government wanted drilling to start and demanded that those opposed to it collected half a million petition signatories to prevent oil exploration in Yasuní. The opposition duly provided over 700,000, but the government cheated and threw out half of the signatures for being supposedly bogus. They were determined to start drilling and did so two years later.

It got a lot worse. Local communities were 'offered' jobs working for the oil industry and bullied into accepting the invasion of territory their ancestry had lived on for generations. Those who resisted were threatened, but also left with few options to make a living. With wildlife scared off their land by the noise of drilling, there was less possibility to hunt and fewer tourists came, preferring to visit untouched areas elsewhere.

Food prices have risen and transport to and from towns is very expensive – up to $80 for a round trip by motorised canoe, which is insane considering how poor these communities are. Diego thinks price rises are deliberate to further isolate anyone not complying with the oil company.

He told me: "They call us unpatriotic and say this is about resources to help the people of Ecuador, but our people were here long before colonisers drew borders, and the forest was here long before mankind."

The government, the oil company and the military all work together in an unholy trinity, making a mockery of promises they made to minimise damage. Diego wanted to show me more of what was happening. Part of me was reluctant at first because I think I wanted to continue my dream jungle experience, but I knew I needed to see the reality. I thought maybe reporting it could lead to some change. I realise now how naïve I was.

The following afternoon, we went by motorised canoe east down the river for several hours. On the way, I saw huge barges transporting diggers and other machinery. They dwarfed our tiny canoe. I felt vulnerable. How can local communities resist in the face of such immense destructive power?

Diego docked the boat and led me a few hundred metres inland to a lagoon. I saw a dead lizard floating on the surface. Diego placed his hand in the water and took out the poor little thing. It was black and covered in oil. He explained to me that oil spills are inevitable, even with careful drilling, but the companies were not being careful at all. Huge areas had been poisoned by crude oil, killing fish and devastating the ecosystem.

He then took me further along the river. Trees and foliage on the river banks were replaced by lights and fencing, and sounds of birds and monkeys replaced by the drone of machines.

It was getting towards dusk. Diego had timed our excursion deliberately because he was very worried about being seen. He told me that locals who try to expose the devastation are regularly threatened.

We docked in a sheltered spot with overhanging trees and then hiked inland. He wanted to show me the road – a road that according to the government and the oil company does not even exist. They had promised to create only 'ecological trails' as part of the oil exploration, but it was just one of many broken promises.

We hiked through dense jungle. I could feel the mosquitoes everywhere and doused my arms and legs in repellent, but they were eating me alive! After half an hour, I could hear the sound of trucks. We emerged next to a road as wide as any found in the towns. I looked up the road that stretched for miles to the east, deeper into the jungle. Either side of the road there were tree stumps. We could see how much of the forest had been cleared to make way for the road.

I took some photos, but I wasn't thinking about what

I was doing at all and my flash lit up our position. I heard a shout. Diego swore and pulled me by the arm. "Guardias!" The guards had seen us. We raced back into the jungle, crashing through foliage, and got back to the boat in minutes. I was terrified.

Diego started the engine and we were away. I thought I could breathe again, but we heard shouts from the riverbank. The guards had reached it and they were armed. One of them aimed his rifle at us, only for the man next to him to raise his hand and stop him from firing. We were close enough that he could easily have shot us.

Diego apologised over and over again on the way back. He was shocked and had not expected to be seen. He kept muttering, "Me conocen" –'they know me'. I knew it was my fault though. My camera flash gave us away. I've never been so relieved to get back to the lodge, where I thought we'd be safe.

I couldn't sleep. Alone in my cabin with a chorus of insects, which the previous night sounded entrancing but now sounded ominous. There were occasional bird calls echoing through the forest. I felt as if the birds were calling out to me in warning.

In the middle of the night, I heard shouting. I went to the cabin window and saw flashlights. Someone was coming. I peeked through the shutters. There were lights in the main lodge building where the community had their meals. I heard more shouting, then a gunshot. Oh my god, please tell me they haven't shot anyone!

It seemed an age before I heard anything else, but then I saw flashlights leading away from the lodge. They were leaving. I waited to be sure they were gone before rushing out of my cabin and up to the lodge. I was terrified they had shot Diego.

I found him lying on the terrace floor moaning, with two women kneeling beside him. His face was bloodied and his leg was lying at an odd angle. I asked if he'd been shot. The woman dressing his wounds shook her head. That was a huge relief, but he'd been badly beaten and his leg looked broken.

He saw me and beckoned me over. He whispered to me that I must not write about what I'd seen or publish any photos. They'd given him a warning. Next time it would be a bullet, he said. He moaned and cried that he might never be able to play football again, which he loved to do on the riverbanks. It broke my heart.

I went back to Coca a few hours later at dawn. I needed to write down what happened, but I made a promise not to publish it. I don't want to put Diego or anyone else in more danger. It puts me in an impossible position. People need to know what's going on, but I don't know how we can stop this. I feel so powerless.

The blog post ends there. Looking at the published posts, Christina had published the first half of this post but only the good parts of her trip. There was nothing about threats to the villagers, the trip upstream to the oil sites or what happened to Diego.

I recall Christina told me over email that she'd gone to the edge of Yasuní and enjoyed seeing the wildlife. She also told me she didn't like Coca and it was sad what the oil industry was doing, but she said nothing about the threats and the violence. I'm sure she didn't want me to worry unnecessarily because she'd got out of that area as soon as things became dangerous. If she had told me, I would have probably wanted her to come home.

I'm back to bargaining and regrets again.

Chapter 14

"You're so selfish sometimes!" You stormed back into the kitchen and started clattering around, banging cupboards, then scrubbing at a dirty pan. You often used to do that when we fought – tidy and clean up. Maybe you just wanted to find some order to help you calm down.

I knew when to leave you alone. We'd been through this so many times. I'd follow you and try to make amends, then you'd glare at me, frowning and scowling. It was always better to wait until later to talk to you again.

You thought I spent too much time working. You wanted me to take some time off so we could go to Ecuador together. I was in the middle of covering an important court case. I wanted you to wait a while or make a shorter trip. Tropical heat and bugs weren't my idea of a holiday anyway; I wince when I remember I said that to you. I was thinking about myself and my needs, not yours.

Did I take you for granted? Did you go because you

needed to get away from me? No, that can't be true because you wanted me to come with you, but I didn't. I was a fool.

I hope you knew how much I loved you. I'm so sorry. Maybe I didn't show it as much after we'd been together so long. It's too late to tell you now. Here I am talking to an urn of your ashes that I can't even bear to scatter because that would be too final a goodbye.

When I'm at home, these thoughts creep back. It's the guilt that tears me apart the most. Sometimes it has a life of its own, like a demon tormenting me. Sadness by comparison is almost comforting. At least it's a simple emotion compared with guilt, which will destroy me if I let it.

When I'm busy out and about, these thoughts disappear for a while. Work is becoming a refuge, an escape from all these emotions, but only temporarily. I worry that I will never be free of this guilt.

My phone is ringing. It's Steve.

"Morning, mate. I know it's last minute but there's a big Extinction Rebellion protest today. I'm going to cover it and the editor said you should probably go along."

"Really? Seems a bit outside my remit."

"Well, there are always arrests so it's bound to be a crime story. There are rumours online about a possible far-right march in the city too. The police will have to try to keep them apart because it could turn nasty."

"A possible riot then. How can I say no? Let me

know when and where we're meeting."

"Eleven a.m., outside Buck House. Another thing – the news desk wants me to look into the South American links to these killings from an environmental point of view. I need to pitch it carefully without the company names. Obviously, we can't come across as condoning or excusing the killings, but there's an important eco-angle here. Let's get our heads together about it."

"Okay. Definitely needs looking into. That could help my own investigation too."

"That's what I was thinking."

I may as well go to the march. Protests make good stories, although I'm on the fence about a load of white middle-class eco-warriors having a go at sabotage. Blockading the right-wing media though, that left me amused, particularly when the papers talked of how 'horrified' their readers were when they couldn't get their daily dose of bile. I'm all for defending freedom of speech but annoying Middle England into turning a deeper shade of beetroot red can't be a bad thing.

I used to love a good protest, but I've learnt to take more care. I nearly got bottled while covering a riot a few years ago. There's no denying there's something infectious about all that righteous indignation though. Maybe I can feed off it and shut out these voices for a while. After being stuck in this flat for months, now I can't wait for any excuse to get out.

It's a sunny day, thankfully. I meet Steve in St James' Park opposite Buckingham Palace. He's chatting to a group of teenagers, scribbling down quotes and totally in his element. Hundreds of people are carrying green XR banners and a drumming group is pummelling away to dancing and cheering.

Steve greets me with a grin. "Welcome to the revolution!"

I smile at that. "Nice thought."

He shrugs and claps me on the shoulder. "Gotta stay optimistic, mate."

I've already put in a call to the Met and they're taking the threat of a clash between rival protests seriously. The police are out in force and I see a dozen officers jog past.

The march heads off through the park to Trafalgar Square. It's a colourful parade with plenty of humour. 'This is no way to treat your mother' reads one banner, with an image of Mother Earth. One woman is dressed up as 'The statue of taking liberties', and a middle-aged man sports a big false belly and a top hat with 'City fat cat' written on it.

When we reach Trafalgar Square, the drumming stops and the protest falls eerily silent. A dozen figures in red glide silently past, arms outstretched, their faces painted white. These are the Red Rebels, turning the carnival atmosphere suddenly sombre. They make their way slowly up towards the National Gallery.

Three barrels are tipped up and red dye poured down the steps beneath a banner reading 'Genocide = ecocide'. On the steps, there are protesters lying down, playing dead. It feels too close to home for me and I find myself looking away.

The speeches start and a young man in a slick suit gets up and reads out a manifesto. He's well-spoken, eloquent and no doubt got his eye on a political career.

Steve nudges me. "News desk just called. There may be trouble brewing in the city. There's a protest outside the banks and the far right are marching that way from Aldgate."

We jump in a cab and reach the Bank of England. Some XR protesters have a truck with a hose. A young mixed-race man with shoulder-length dreadlocks starts spraying the outside of the building with red paint. A woman on top of the truck gets out a megaphone and starts a speech: "We need to stop the banks funding ecocide and genocide. No more blood money!"

There's shouting from behind me. A crowd with union jack banners is marching straight towards us. I instinctively move back to the kerb and Steve follows.

A skinhead in a sleeveless top with tattoos down both arms shouts, "Oi, brown boy! If you don't like the pound, why don't you piss off to where you come from?"

The man with the hose turns and looks at him for a moment.

"I come from London, mate."

The skinhead swears at him.

The protester shakes his head and smiles. "You look like Snow White, mate. You need some colour!"

I watch open-mouthed as he turns the hose on the

skinhead, taking him completely by surprise and drenching him in red paint. It's not a pretty sight.

All hell breaks loose as the far-right mob surround the truck. There are a dozen of them and only a handful of XR protesters. The guy in dreadlocks drops the hose and raises his arms in a combat stance. He clearly knows how to handle himself. The skinhead rushes at him and gets a kung fu kick to the chest. Two more rush at him. There are too many of them. They're punching and kicking him. He hits the deck. I take one look at Steve and he's thinking the same as me: this guy could get killed.

Suddenly, a police van screeches to a halt next to the protesters' truck and a riot squad gets out. They pull the rioters off the guy on the floor. To my relief, he gets up groggily. He's got a bloody nose and is holding his ribs, but still has plenty of fight in him. "Come on then, white boy. You're too much of a pussy to fight me yourself. Need your boyfriends?"

Two of the riot squad hold him back while two others get hold of the skinhead who first challenged him. The mob aren't moving back though, far from it. A bottle smashes a few metres in front of us. One of them shouts, "What you protecting him for? Let him go, we'll take him."

The police put the skinhead and the man in dreadlocks into separate vans. The riot squad get their shields and form a line, separating the two sides. There's a tense standoff for a few minutes, but eventually the mob starts moving back. Things start to calm down.

When it's clear the action is over, I head down to Liverpool Street police station where the men have been taken. The guy with the hose is named Abel Jackson, his assailant Lee Norris.

The police move quickly on the case as footage is already on the internet. Someone filmed the whole incident. Norris is charged with actual bodily harm and the police are hunting more of his gang, who were caught on camera fighting. Jackson is charged with vandalism and common assault. Apparently hosing someone with paint counts as assault. I'm not sure about that decision.

A crowd has gathered outside the station as word gets round about the charges. They're chanting, "Justice for Jackson!" He gets bail and comes out the front to a chorus of cheers. He raises a fist and smiles before getting into a car. He's enjoying the attention.

Extinction Rebellion is quick to release a statement: "We deplore the violence at today's protest and especially the despicable racist abuse suffered by our members. Although there is no doubt Mr Jackson was provoked, we cannot condone any form of violence. We pride ourselves on training our members in de-escalation. Therefore, we can confirm that Abel Jackson is expelled from XR with immediate effect."

Steve thinks it's fair enough. "XR is walking a tightrope at present. There are plenty in the government who'd like to classify them as anti-capitalist terrorists and lock them up. Incidents like this won't help if they're serious about keeping it peaceful."

I file a report on the clash to the news desk and it's one of the lead stories of the day: 'Mixed-race eco-activist attacked by far-right gang after hosing down skinhead.' The video makes for compulsive viewing too.

London is a troubled city at present and something tells me this is far from over. I feel there is more trouble brewing.

Chapter 15

I haven't been awake long when my phone buzzes. Private number: "Check email. Urgent." It must be him again. I go to the laptop and open an email entitled 'Manifesto'. It's a link to a video.

The video begins soaring over a rainforest with a voiceover. There's some kind of distortion on the voice. "The Amazon jungle, the world's greatest source of biodiversity, a sacred place for millennia, now ravaged to the point of total destruction by greed.

"Arson…" The video shows footage of an enormous forest fire. "Deforestation…" A huge tree crashes down. "Oil…" The video shows pools of black. "Mining…" A huge digger ploughs through a riverbank.

"These are just some of the industries, led by corporations and backed by governments, destroying what is sacred." The footage cuts to images of business leaders and politicians shaking hands.

"And what of those who resist? Fear, intimidation and murder." The video shows bodies at the bottom of a ravine and a close-up of a dead indigenous man, his head soaked in blood.

"Four environmentalists a week are killed by greed." More images of indigenous protesters flash past. 'IT'S TIME TO EVEN UP THE SCORE'. These words flash across the screen in red.

The video cuts to images of skyscrapers and the stock exchange. "London: birthplace of the extractionist, colonial economy and cradle of capitalism. One of the world's most corrupt cities, a haven for money launderers and those who fund murder.

"To these criminals we say: you may not have pulled the trigger, but you supplied the guns. We will target those who work for corporations that pollute and kill."

The video cuts to the word 'oil' from the first crime scene, then a split-second shot of Blakely in the car. 'Timber', the word scratched into the beam, and a fleeting shot of Grover hanging. 'Beef', written in bloody meat juice, and the worst photo of all: an image of Liu's head twisted back horrifically.

"And not only these industries. Mining, clothing and the bankers who move the money – you are all on our list.

"Our crimes are minuscule compared with yours. Change, repent and stop destroying what must be preserved. This is a prayer for the twenty-first century. Don't make it a requiem."

The video shows the mural from the photograph found with Blakely's body, then cuts to an animated image of green shoots growing, the leaves covered in blood.

'Out of their ashes, green shoots will grow' is written across the screen.

The video ends.

I sit back and blow a long breath out. These people mean business and I seem to be caught in the middle of some kind of eco-jihad.

I go back through the video frame by frame. I'm sure there was something I missed. I get to the part where it mentions four environmentalists killed per week. The cuts to different shots are quick, but I stop at one and see that my mind wasn't playing tricks on me. It's a photo of Christina. I enlarge it. She's talking to some indigenous children. I recognise it from her blog.

This must be a personal message to me and it's clear what it's saying: Christina was killed for her environmentalism. My head is spinning. Who the hell are these people and how do they know so much about my wife?

I go back to scanning the rest of the video and stare at the image of green shoots. Then it hits me. I can't believe I've been so blind. What are underneath shoots? Roots of course. It's *him*. He's not just involved; I think he's behind all of this.

I get up and pace around the flat. I've been led on a merry dance by a mass murderer. I can't process all this right now.

I phone the news desk at the paper and the duty news editor Richard tells me they've been sent the video along with all media outlets. Apparently, it was taken down from YouTube but keeps reappearing on other channels. The video has received over a million hits in just a few hours. It's all over the news. No first bite for me from Root this time then. That's almost a relief. I don't want tip-offs from him if this is all his doing.

I check the main news channels and the media is in meltdown with headlines like: 'Crazed killers target London businesses', 'Eco-terrorists admit revenge killings in gruesome video', 'Amazon avengers terrorise London'.

Amazon avengers – seriously? The tabloids can't resist their alliteration and nicknames. I check the Met press releases and they refer to the case as the 'Green Shoots killings', so that's how I will refer to it.

My phone rings. It's Steve. "Hi, John. I presume you've seen the video?"

"Yes, he sent it to me directly. What I feared must be true – this guy is no private investigator, he's up to his neck in it, and he's had me dancing to his tune."

"What? How do you mean?"

"Well, I first broke the story. I reckon he was using me to get as much coverage as possible."

"If that's true then he doesn't need you for that anymore. The story's a monster now."

I need to tell Steve what I've discovered. I figure I need a sounding board, otherwise this will drive me crazy.

"There's something else, Steve. Christina was on that

video. It was a fleeting image but it was there – a picture of her in Ecuador. I had to slow it right down to check."

"What? Are you sure? I didn't see that. That must have really shook you up."

"And then some. I don't know what to make of it."

"Do you think this guy was involved in her death? It might explain why he knows so much about it."

"I hadn't thought of that, but no, that's not my gut feeling. Her photo appeared when the video talked about environmentalists being killed."

Steve swears under this breath. "I don't know what to say."

There's nothing I'd like better than to never hear from this Root again. It's way out of my comfort zone, but he keeps feeding me clues on what happened to Christina and I keep taking the bait.

"Steve, there's something else I haven't told you. I think he's been following me. A few days ago, after the press conference, he texted me to say that I asked a good question."

"It went out live though. Maybe he heard the question on TV?"

"He also said I was looking better."

"Oh. That's creepy as hell."

"Yeah, but if he's behind all this, I wouldn't be surprised if he turned up to watch the press conference. He likes playing games."

"Have you told the police? It wouldn't be the first time you've had to get protection, John."

"No. I didn't say any more to them than that I'd had anonymous tip-offs. I think Morrison is pissed at me for being ahead of her department on this."

"I think you should tell them about it. If this guy is involved then his contact with you could be of use to the investigation."

"I'm aware of that."

I know Steve is right about the police, and I've been turning that over in my mind, but my priority is finding out the truth about Christina. Root must know more than he's let on, but if the police start looking into all our communications, I may never hear from him again. Or worse, contacting the police could annoy him, and considering what he's capable of, that would be unwise.

I feel like a starving animal being led on a trail of scraps into a forest. A dangerous forest too, but then I figure, what the hell do I have to lose? Part of me is dead already. The love of my life is gone. How much I care about my own life, I honestly don't know anymore. I may as well follow the scraps to see where they lead.

Chapter 16

I'd had too much to drink that night, as usual. You told me once that you thought I liked being a journalist more for the boozy nights than for the job itself. You hated it when I was roaring drunk too, which really rained on my parade.

I wondered if you came with me to the office Christmas party at that pub in Farringdon to keep an eye on me. It had been quite a fun night until we were getting ready to leave. Fiona from features sidled up to me completely drunk. She placed her hand on my chest and asked where I thought I was going. I smiled at her sheepishly. She'd always been a bit flirty. I thought I took her hand away, but maybe I didn't. You glared at me and stormed out.

By the time I got my coat, you'd gone. I found you back at the flat after I hailed a cab. At first you were quiet and ignored my apologies, slapping away my attempts at a hug. Then you let rip – how I didn't respect you, and if I wanted some London media slut, I should go and get one. How I didn't even want a baby and that's why I kept saying we should wait until next year.

None of it seemed fair to me. Maybe it was fair in your mind. You couldn't see much difference between drunken banter and cheating. To you, it was all the same slippery slope. You used to tell me how your dad's claims of 'working late' were never such thing and how your ma always knew he was out with another woman. You said that Latin men cheated like it was a national sport. I could see the scars it left on you, scars that opened at any sign that I was going to stray.

I never cheated on you, never even came close, but it didn't matter how many times I said that. I could tell there was always the thought in your head that you couldn't shake – that one day it would happen.

I found it a ridiculous idea. You, the stunner who turned heads every time you walked into a bar, and me, the scrawny, tousle-haired geek who could never get a girlfriend at school. Friends told me I was the cat that got the cream when I met you, and they were right.

No, it wasn't fair but I forgave you. I didn't give you all you deserved though. You were wrong about the baby. It's not that I didn't want children. Of course I did, but it scared me. I didn't know if I'd be any good at it. I'd seen friends like Steve settle down with kids and their lives changed totally. I wasn't ready, but I was getting there. I should have manned up and started a family with you. Now it's too late.

I need to throw myself back into work to push these thoughts away for a while. Steve has been working on an extended feature looking at the conflicts caused by the extraction of raw materials in Latin America. He's emailed over a draft.

It makes grim reading. I knew some of the troubled history of oil exploration in Ecuador, and Christina's blog had revealed more, but it's far worse than I'd imagined. According to Steve, since drilling began in the Ecuadorian Amazon in the 1960s, millions of barrels of oil have either leaked or been dumped into the surrounding forest. Oil companies have been fighting indigenous groups for decades in courts, and when a company actually lost a landmark case, instead of paying up, they simply appealed endlessly and spent millions in legal fees to avoid paying billions in compensation.

The areas around Lago Agrio and Coca have been particularly badly affected, and it's not only Ecuador but a similar story in Peru and Colombia. Steve has investigated the company that first victim Blakely worked for and it's active in both Ecuador and Peru, but he's treading carefully and avoiding any accusations. Oil companies have teams of very expensive lawyers, after all.

The situation with timber and cattle ranching is in some ways even worse because it involves clearing the forest completely. Illegal logging is rife, and legal logging is hardly any better because local governments designate logging rights on lands that have belonged to indigenous peoples for generations. There is a system in place where imports to Europe have to be certified as sustainably sourced, but Steve's investigations have found these certifications are often not even worth the paper they're written on. Companies simply pay off officials and rainforest timber magically becomes legitimate and 'sustainable', ending up in European furniture stores.

The farmers and ranchers use forest fires to clear vast areas of rainforest to grow palm oil or raise cattle for beef, dairy and leather. Steve has found examples of Amazon tribes that have simply disappeared overnight, unable to escape the terrifying speed of forest fires. The demand for beef worldwide is enormous and most is exported to buyers who don't ask questions about its origin, particularly in North America and China. This may help explain the targeting of Liu.

As Christina wrote on her blog, it's depressing and the destruction seems unstoppable. I wonder how Steve stays so upbeat reporting on it all, but he has found something more optimistic. He's been looking into the photograph of the mural found with Blakely and its slogan *De sus cenizas, crecerán brotes verdes*. We both know it is key to the case because the translation has become in effect a mission statement for the killings.

Steve has been in touch with several South American-based reporters and uncovered a photograph on the web that looks identical. There's very little information alongside the photo except that it is in a town called Mitú near the Colombian border with Brazil. Steve has asked Richie McGill, a freelance reporter who covers Colombia and neighbouring Ecuador, to look into it.

"It's time to even up the score." Those words from the video keep echoing in my mind. I'm beginning to understand these must be revenge killings, but I don't see how bumping off a few businessmen in London is going to make a difference to what's happening on the other side of the world.

There's something else from Steve. He's sent me a separate email to his draft article.

Hi John,

I found this news report about unexplained deaths of indigenous leaders in Ecuador from a few months ago. The timing raised alarm bells and a foreigner is mentioned in the report. I think you need to look into it.

Let's talk about it more. I really want to help in any way I can.

Steve

The attached news report from a site named *Acción Ecológica* is in Spanish. I sift through it and use a translator for some unfamiliar words. It reports on the deaths of four indigenous leaders near Lago Agrio in Ecuador. They apparently all died within a day of each other following a community meeting. The article claims their community was resisting mining. The final line of the article reads: 'There are unconfirmed reports that a European woman staying in the village also died.'

I re-read that several times. I check the date of the report and it's from October, the week after Christina died. The report could be referring to her.

I already doubted the diagnosis of dengue fever, but this could be proof. There's no way five people would die of dengue within hours of each other. Something else must have happened out there.

Chapter 17: DCI Morrison

DCI Morrison was first in the meeting room. She wanted to get all her ducks in a row because the super was getting edgy about the lack of progress so far on the Green Shoots case. Morrison needed to get something concrete, and fast, so she was pleased to have a lead on Blakely at least.

Superintendent Harman entered the room, locked in quiet conversation with a man Morrison didn't recognise. She waited for the rest of the investigation team to sit, then launched into her presentation using a projector.

"First, I'll go through a summary of the evidence we have so far on each of the three Green Shoots victims, mentioning common factors between them, then I'll discuss next priority actions.

"The first victim, Keith Blakely, had enough sedative in his system for us to be reasonably certain he was already unconscious when he died of carbon monoxide poisoning. We still have four days unaccounted for between the last sighting of him in the Bloomsbury

Whisky Tavern on the evening of 19th Feb and when he was found on 23rd Feb.

"We talked to the bar manager and something came up that we're looking into further. The usual barman, Jack Murphy, was down to work that night but he didn't go in. He claims to have received a message about a shift mix-up. As yet we don't know who was working behind the bar, so enquiries are ongoing. We talked to other customers and one recalls seeing someone matching Blakely's description chatting at the bar. He was a regular there apparently. We got a description of a man talking with him – tall, short dark hair and glasses. We are working on a sketch because out of the three cases, it's the only possible sighting of a suspect."

Morrison paused to let this news sink in. It was a major development.

She continued. "On the Jeremy Grover killing, we have far less to go on. He left work as normal around five forty-five p.m. on 28th Feb, but he was not found until 5th March. Pathology estimates he'd been dead no more than three days, which means, like Blakely, there are several days unaccounted for. We found faeces and urine in the warehouse, which indicated he'd been kept there for some time. Marks on his wrists are consistent with being restrained. So, like Blakely, the murder was made to look like suicide.

"The third victim, Gang Liu, was last seen the evening before he was found, so the time frame is far narrower. He left an office in the West End around five thirty p.m. on 10th March. We picked him up on CCTV walking through Leicester Square, from where we think he walked to Romilly Street. As yet, we have no witnesses that saw him enter the building in Romilly Street. It's of note that Mr Liu had the same sedative in his body that we found in Keith Blakely, and traces were found in his food. Liu would most likely have been unconscious when beef was forced down his throat, killing him."

Morrison looked away briefly as the projector behind her showed the gruesome photograph of Liu.

"Apart from use of the same sedative, there are other parallels between victims. They all worked in raw material industries active in the third world – oil, timber and beef – and, according to the now infamous video, this is why they were targeted. We are looking into their precise job roles to see if there may be more specific reasons why these men, and their companies, were chosen.

"A key point: we have discovered that all three victims reported a phone lost or stolen in the weeks before their deaths. It appears they all obtained new phones quickly, which is no surprise. However, no phones were found with the bodies. We believe the victims may have been targeted and tracked through their phones, so we are looking into their phone records in more detail.

"So, priority actions: check all three victims' phone records, follow up on Blakely witnesses in the bar to get a suspect sketch, and keep working CCTV for all three crimes."

Morrison looked at the super to indicate she was finished. DS Harman glanced around, then gestured to the man sitting next to him. "Thank you, DCI Morrison. I should have done this earlier, but I'd like to introduce Special Agent Mike Edmunds from Counter Terrorism. He'll be working closely with us on the case from now on."

Edmunds stood up. "Okay, everyone. I'll cut to the chase. You all know how big this case is, and I'm here to make sure we cover all angles. It's quite clear not only are we dealing with an organised murder campaign, but a well-orchestrated media campaign too. We're currently analysing the video content in detail, but we also need to talk about the flow of information."

He paused pointedly.

"DS Harman has some concerns about certain members of the media and how they are privy to information. I share these concerns. The last thing we need in this type of investigation, particularly now it's a matter of national security, is loose talk to the media."

Morrison opened her mouth to interject but Edmunds held up his hand and continued. "Now, I'm not saying there are leaks from here, but the fact is that sensitive information is somehow finding its way into the media. DCI Morrison, what can you tell me about dealings with journalists so far, in particular with a certain John Adamson from *The Sentinel*?"

Morrison was wrong-footed. She hadn't expected this from Edmunds. "I've known John Adamson a long time and he's a sharp reporter. He has quite a reputation and I'm used to him coming at me with tip-offs that are on the nose, but in this case, it has raised alarm bells. He broke the story in the first place and seemed to guess it was foul play even before the evidence confirmed it. He also knew forensic details that had not been released to the media. Now, I trust my team, so if he isn't getting it from us…"

Edmunds completed her sentence: "Then who is he getting it from? It wouldn't be the first time terrorists have contacted the media directly. I want to know more about this John Adamson. We may need to talk to him."

Edmunds turned to the super, who brought the meeting to a close. DCI Morrison made her way out, deep in thought.

Chapter 18: Shawcross

Shawcross was in a good mood. Business was booming, particularly from the big wholesalers. It turned out the board's fears that synthetic materials might threaten the leather market had proven far too pessimistic. Shawcross was pleased with himself for seeing the opportunities in Brazil, despite the misgivings of a few whiney liberals in the boardroom.

He figured he could treat himself because he'd been good. It turned out his luck was holding too. She'd been fully booked this evening but an email popped up on his phone informing him a slot had become available.

Shawcross smiled to himself, glancing around the office. He turned off the company Wi-Fi on his phone and made the booking on his own data. He couldn't be too careful – accessing this kind of site on company time wasn't wise. They'd probably forgive him though, given the business he generated.

Mistress Sahara was the best he'd come across in New York, and he'd sampled many of Manhattan's finest. She was firm and kept him right on that tantalising edge between agony and ecstasy to keep him booking at least once a month. He occasionally tried a new lady, but Sahara was his favourite.

As he exited his downtown office onto a busy street, he breathed in the scent of hot dogs and onions from a street vendor. They smelt delicious but he would wait to eat. It was more satisfying to work up an appetite. That would be his reward.

He hailed a cab uptown. He'd been taking taxis more often since being robbed on the subway a few weeks ago. He loved New York but it had its fair share of scumbags. He'd never even seen the guy either. How he'd love to beat him to a pulp.

"Let's get ready to rumble!" The boxing commentary inside the taxi was lame. It was just a cab ride, not fight night. The driver saw him roll his eyes and turned it off. "Sorry, sir, but the tourists love it, ya know?" Yes, he knew and didn't begrudge it much. After all, tourists shopping in Manhattan made him a lot of money.

Shawcross loosened his tie. It was hot. The cabby straightened the rear-view mirror. "Would you like the air-con on, sir?"

Shawcross nodded and untucked his shirt. He wished he could wear it that way all the time. It would hide the flab of his belly. He should have time for a shower in the hotel room before she arrived. She demanded he was clean for her. She was always very demanding, just the way he liked it.

He arrived at 86th street and tipped the driver an

extra ten, as he was feeling generous. Central Park View Hotel was a solid option – good enough to fit the bill, but not so top-of-the-range that his colleagues or clients might frequent it. That would be awkward. He smiled at the thought.

He gave his name to reception, handed over the credit card and took his key. The receptionist barely looked up. She looked familiar, and cute too. He might ask her to join him for a drink some time, although she'd no doubt refuse if she remembered how often he took a room there. Bitches can be so judgemental sometimes.

Shawcross took a shower and sat on the bed in his briefs. Patting his belly, he made a mental note to get back to the gym next week. He looked over at the clock. 7.05 p.m. He frowned; she was never late. He picked up the hotel phone, but just as he was about to dial, there was a knock at the door. That was weird. Reception usually called to let him know his 'therapist' was on her way.

He opened the door. A woman with shoulder-length red hair met his gaze steadily. Not Sahara.

"Where…?"

Before he could say more, she cut him off. "Mistress Sahara regrets she cannot attend this evening due to an unforeseen urgent matter, the details of which are none of your business." She paused, staring at him and widening her eyes.

"I am her associate Atacama and have been fully briefed on your needs. Mistress Sahara has also

115

instructed as a courtesy, your next session will be at a fifty per cent discount, including VIP extras."

She paused. "Unless you wish to cancel this evening?" She placed a hand on her hip and gave him a piercing look.

Shawcross considered it for a moment. He'd already paid for the room and couldn't argue with the special rate and extras for next time. This one was good too. Striking. The hair was probably a wig, but those cold blue eyes and high cheekbones got his blood pumping. Her long black coat was open, revealing a full PVC bodysuit and thigh-high boots. She flexed her black leather gloves.

He stood aside and invited her in. Atacama wasted no time in ordering him to lie face up and she produced four sets of cuffs, shackling his hands and feet to the metal bed frame.

"I'm sorry if I was rude earlier," Shawcross said, watching as she took several candles from a black leather bag and placed them in a candelabra. She lit each one, before turning to him and saying, "You will be."

The hot wax was perfect. Delicious pain as it dripped onto his toes. Atacama slowly worked her way up to the tops of his thighs.

"What do you say?"

"Thank you, mistress," he gasped.

She put the candelabra on the table and returned to her bag.

"Mistress Sahara asked me to bring something for

you. You are instructed to wear it this evening and keep it for next time."

She produced a leather mask. Shawcross beamed at her. "A gift, how kind!"

"Sahara is not kind at all. It is part of your punishment for past misdemeanours."

Shawcross heard the strains of music. A deep voice was singing of loneliness and torture. Shawcross smiled and sank back into the pillow.

She fit the mask over his head and drew it at the neck so only his eyes and mouth were visible. Shawcross was surprised at how tight the mask was. The eye holes seemed to be covered with transparent film.

Just as he thought about using his safe word, Atacama peeled down his shorts and he braced himself. Then she got off the bed and stood next to him, with her hands on her hips. "Tell me, what is the mask made from?"

Shawcross breathed in deeply. There was no mistaking it.

"Leather."

"You love leather, don't you? Say it!"

"I love leather."

"Not loud enough." She put one hand down to her side. For a brief instant, Shawcross thought he saw a flash.

"I love leather!"

"Again. What do you love?"

"LEATHER!" he shouted.

She smiled at him. "Good, then more leather you shall have."

She produced a belt and lifted his head, tying it tight around his neck over the mask.

Shawcross felt something was wrong. This was not how Sahara handled him.

Atacama returned to her bag and lent over him. "Open wide."

He was about to protest but she shoved a cloth inside. It had a strong chemical smell. Shawcross felt immediately woozy.

Atacama closed the mouth zip and tightened the belt. Shawcross couldn't breathe. He thrashed around on the bed, heaving his chest.

Atacama looked at him disdainfully. The chemicals sapped his remaining strength, and with one final jolt of his limbs, he fell silent.

Atacama took out lipstick and crossed to the ensuite bathroom to write, as instructed. She then took a blade from her bag and found Shawcross's black leather shoes. She cut away strips and arranged them on the bedside table, as instructed. She exited the room and went down the stairs and out of the fire escape at the rear of the hotel. She paused in the alleyway to text a single 'X', as instructed, and made her way into the Manhattan night.

Chapter 19

Things have been as crazy as I predicted after that video was released. The 'manifesto' singled out mining, clothing and banking on the hit list, so people working in those sectors are understandably nervous, and there are reports of higher than usual employee absences. The London stock market has fallen sharply too. There's a climate of fear similar to when terrorists were targeting London with bombs. The Green Shoots investigation has now become a counter-terrorism operation. DCI Morrison is still involved, but MI5 are too. The whole situation feels surreal.

It's about to get even more surreal. I've received an email from 'rootsmusicNYC' entitled 'Start spreading the news'.

There's a single image attached, named 'manhattanunmasked.jpg'. I take a deep breath, as I know what's coming. It's another body, this time a man naked except for briefs, handcuffed to a bed. He's wearing a black mask and there's something in his mouth. It looks like a cloth.

NYC, Sinatra lyrics, Manhattan – there are enough clues to know this must be in New York, not London. He's branching out then. I recall that transatlantic twang to his voice when he called me, so it's not a complete surprise.

I check the main news sites in New York, but there's nothing. I go back to the photo and zoom in to see if there are any further clues. On the bedside table there is a placemat. I zoom in further and find what I need. It's branded: 'Central Park View Hotel'.

I call the news desk to find out who we have in New York. Carol Taylor, it turns out, so I leave a voicemail for her. I don't have any contacts in NYPD so it's best to leave it with her.

Carol gets back to me a couple of hours later. She tells me NYPD were tight-lipped initially, but eventually confirmed a man had been found dead. The hotel no doubt wanted to keep it quiet, afraid of bad publicity.

Carol also found that NYPD were unaware of the spate of killings in London and hadn't put two and two together. That's not a total surprise considering how US-focused the media is across the pond.

She sends over details. His name was Martin Shawcross, aged 48. He worked in purchasing in the fashion industry. She managed to confirm from the police that the hallmark messages were left at the scene. The 'mission statement' was written in what appeared to be green lipstick on the bathroom mirror, the word 'leather' was spelt out with strips of leather, and it seems he was asphyxiated with leather too. It follows the Green Shoots pattern in every aspect.

More interestingly, there is a lead on a suspect for the first time. NYPD are searching for a red-haired woman seen by a hotel employee at Shawcross's door.

A different country and a female suspect – I had presumed there was a man behind this, probably Root himself, but it seems he may have an accomplice. That would make sense, considering how much planning it would take to carry out so many murders.

I decide to put in a call to DCI Morrison to check how the investigation is going. "Hello, John. Yes, we've just had contact from Interpol. I'm still on the case but the assistant chief constable is taking charge, particularly now Counter Terrorism are involved, so I can't give you much of an update I'm afraid."

"Right. Understood."

"Your name came up yesterday, as it happens."

"Oh, how's that?"

"Well, my superiors are wondering how you seem to be one step ahead of us much of the time, and so am I, in fact. Interpol said the media had already got wind of the death in New York. I'm guessing that was you?"

"Actually no, it was my colleague Carol in New York. I did say before that I've been receiving anonymous tip-offs, Denise."

"Are they anonymous though, John? This has become a national security issue. If you know the source then it could be crucial to our investigation."

"I honestly don't know who is sending me this information."

There's silence on the line, then she says tersely, "I'm sure we'll be in touch again soon, John."

Morrison hangs up. She's a lot frostier than usual, and it sounds like she doesn't trust me anymore, which is annoying considering the good will we've built up over the years. Her instincts are right though. I do know more and I should probably tell her, but I'm mindful it may be the last I hear from Root if I do. I need to make sure I get everything from him about Christina first.

I receive another email from Carol informing me that photos of victim Martin Shawcross have been leaked on the internet. She's already contacted NYPD, who have confirmed these are not police photos. They are graphic and have been taken off many sites, but she's sent me screenshots.

There's the trademark twisted humour: in a photo captioned 'Before' on the left, Shawcross is alive. He's in the mask with only his eyes and mouth visible. He looks to be shouting with a crazed look in his eyes. I wonder if he knew he was going to die at that point. On the right is another photo captioned 'After'. It's the same photo I received of Shawcross's body.

Carol and I file a report quickly, leading with, 'Green Shoots now global murder hunt'. I check the news online and what was mainly a British story is now making the news worldwide. Most major US TV networks are covering it.

The seediness of Shawcross's death makes it even more appetising for the media. There are hysterical headlines like, 'Suffocation sex game death part of anti-capitalist murder spree'. The leak of the photos only feeds the grotesque fascination.

As I'm reading through the coverage, I get a text from Steve telling me to check my email. It's a web link with just one line from Steve: 'Rupert has really excelled himself this time!'

I click on a link to *Free People News*. It's an opinion piece.

It's time to clamp down on ALL eco-terrorists

London is living in fear yet again. If it's not Irish or Muslim terrorists, now the city has to deal with yet another murderous group with a twisted 'cause' to justify their actions.

Green Shoots, Amazon Avengers – call them what you will. Whoever these people are, they are murderers of innocent businessman who have done nothing more than do what makes this country and this city great – work hard to make a living.

There has been a lot of chat online about the targeting of certain companies from the usual left-wing loons who want to excuse what has happened. Listening to some of these deluded whingers, anybody would think we should all crawl back into the jungle from where our ancestors came millennia ago. Yes, it's brilliant that you ride a bike and buy sustainable, recyclable, fair trade, organic bamboo furniture; great that you've gone vegan and have a solar-powered roof; but not everyone in Britain has the money to be that choosy – they're too busy making ends meet.

These people seem to forget that the industrial revolution is what made Britain the powerhouse of the world. We should be proud of our combustion engines, not ashamed of them. In fact, our oil companies are doing some of the best work in renewable technology. We all know oil isn't going to last forever, and these companies are doing a lot more for the planet with their research and investment than these sick anarchists.

But it's not just the killings that have to stop. We also need to stop putting up with a bunch of students and their bearded grandads shutting down London in the name of environmental activism. They shower our banks and our historic squares with red paint, as if Britain is to blame for the killing of tribespeople in far-flung lands by their own countrymen. What do they actually want the London banking sector to do? Stop giving vital investment to countless projects around the world that push civilisation forward? And make no mistake – that is exactly what this is about. Do we move forward or go back to some Neanderthal mythical noble savage existence?

It's also about time we stopped the doom and gloom of the climate change hoax. The BBC may think climate change denial is a fringe view, but it is not – the liberal media simply repress the truth to pursue their radical left agenda to give more power to their friends.

We need the police to catch those who are killing our citizens, and now a citizen of our closest ally as well. But just as importantly, we need to clear these eco-extremists off our streets and label them what they are – terrorists. Only then can our wonderful city get back to normal.

I can't stand Hennessy but I've got to admit, he's found his niche. Although his attempt to align with the man in the street seems laughable to me, it will doubtless strike a chord with a lot of readers. Clearly, the whining, liberal *Sentinel* was never his spiritual home and this hard-right rabble-rousing, hippy-bashing rhetoric suits him down to the ground.

It is dangerous, extremist talk though, typical of clickbait opinion pieces looking for shock value and impact. It's one thing to hope these killers are stopped – I can't really argue with that – but trying to put XR and environmental protesters in the same category and labelling them as terrorists? That's on the way to a police state. Steve said it's rumoured there are plenty in the government already pushing for this. This city is ready to explode.

Chapter 20

Once again, the Green Shoots case is taking up too much of my time when I want to be making headway on what happened to Christina. That news report Steve sent across has really shaken me up and I've been thinking of little else. If it is true that several tribal leaders died and the European woman mentioned was Christina, then it wasn't dengue fever that killed her. It was murder.

I haven't read through all of Christina's unpublished blog posts yet. The post on Yasuní clearly showed she was dicing with danger, but that was in a different area of Ecuador. I need to find out more about what she was doing further north.

There's another post in the drafts, dated just two days before she was taken to hospital.

The lost spirits

Today, Sami took me deeper into the jungle. He wanted to show me the tallest ceiba tree in the area. In English, we call it the 'kapok' and I think this derives from the

Kichwa language because 'qapak' means 'mighty'.

Mighty is what these trees are. They can grow over two hundred feet with a span of branches often as wide as they are high, and the roots stretch out over a hundred feet. They look to me like the world's most amazing giant umbrellas. These trees feed the forest, giving life to it, and are home to thousands of species.

We took the canoe further upstream through an area I'd visited before, but it had changed dramatically. There was the noise of machinery in the distance and more trees cut down near the banks. Sami said bitterly that they were building more roads.

After half an hour, we banked the canoe and began hiking. I could still hear the sound of machinery but it was distant. Sami had brought his machete, expecting to find dense undergrowth, but a path had already been cleared. There were tree stumps and logs all around us. It was a question of either stepping over or walking around them, not hacking through them.

It came as a relief to see the giant kapok tree in front of us because for a moment I feared it had also been cut down. I thought Sami would be relieved too but I looked over at him and he was shaking away tears. He told me he'd been making this pilgrimage to the tree since he was a boy. He knew the route through the forest blindfolded but now the kapok tree's friends and companions had been wiped out.

As I looked at the awesome size of the kapok's trunk, Sami pressed his head against it, closed his eyes and listened. He opened them and, no longer hiding his tears, looked at me and said, "They've gone."

He sat down and cried. I didn't know what he meant and I couldn't think what to say so I placed a hand on his shoulder. After some time, he repeated what he'd said, then explained to me that the forest spirits live in the kapok tree. He could sometimes sense them, even hear them, but now he said there was only silence. I cast my eyes around and listened for the sounds of birds, insects and monkeys, but there was only an eerie quiet. It was as if the life of the forest had drained away. Sami made a motion upwards with his hand to indicate the spirits had flown away.

As we made our sad journey back, Sami told me a story his people passed on from generation to generation. I cannot tell it with the same deep understanding as Sami, but I will try to recount it here.

"One day, the tribe was hungry and walked deep into the forest to a river to catch fish. One of the men went to the giant tree to ask Juri, the spirit of the wind and guardian of the river, for permission to fish. Juri refused the request, saying it was not the right time and the people would have to wait until there were enough fish in that part of the river.

"The man told his companions but they refused to listen, driven desperate by hunger after such a long walk. The man was afraid of angering Juri and went back again to speak to the spirit, who once more insisted it was not the time to fish. When he returned to his

companions, he found they had already killed many fish and cooked them on a fire, laughing and eating happily.

"When Juri discovered this disobedience, she became very angry. She told the man who had talked with her to hide in a cave with his family where he would be safe, so he hurried home and hid with his wife and children. Suddenly, the sky grew dark, the wind grew strong and branches of trees began falling. These blinded the people who had been fishing, leaving them unable to find their way home. They were devoured by jaguars and wild boars that emerged from the jungle. The family in the cave were the only ones left of their tribe and they learnt to never again disobey the forest spirits."

After finishing the story, Sami told me the forest is angry at what people are doing and he fears a terrible vengeance across the world – the moving of earth, the howling of wind, the rising of water and the raging of fire. "The earth is becoming hot with fury. If only people revered trees instead of revering a man nailed to a tree, perhaps it would not come to this," Sami said.

I felt a heavy sadness and that feeling stayed with me when we got back to the village. I found a very subdued atmosphere. Even young Marcelo, who was usually happy to see me, looked downcast. He was sitting with some of the women, sullenly cutting vegetables, and he ignored my greeting.

If there's one criticism I have of this community, it's that they really don't accept some men are different, but then I've found that in many parts of Ecuador. Marcelo is effeminate, that much is clear to me. He is struggling with who he really is, but the men joke about him and tell him to spend time with the women. I see how much it hurts him, but I don't feel it's my place to say anything.

Everyone seemed tense though, not just Marcelo. I asked Sami if something had happened in the village and he told me tomorrow there is an important meeting of community leaders in the area. He wasn't sure, but he believed they would discuss making a stand against the mining encroachments on their territory. Sami heard there had been contact with lawyers and talk of going to court, but not everyone was in agreement.

Some of the neighbouring villagers have left to take jobs with mining and oil companies. They are seen as traitors but Sami says he understands them. They want to be safe and everything here is so expensive – transport and particularly education for the children. Most parents here can't afford it but they don't want their children to grow up uneducated and trapped in poverty. Sami also told me some of the leaders fear reprisals and violence against the villagers. "We can't fight guns with spears," Sami said, clenching his fist.

Even more of a concern was what Sami told me about Tonio. He seemed helpful at first, but now I wonder why he warned me about this place. Maybe it wasn't just for my own safety. Tonio said he had a strip of land here earmarked for an eco-lodge, but Sami has since told me

he saw mining employees there and he thought Tonio
acquired it only to get a foothold in the territory for
mining concessions. I honestly don't know how involved
Tonio is, but now I think I was naïve to trust him.

I'm glad the villagers are trying to make a stand, but
I share Sami's concern. I don't know where all this
could lead. It could be dangerous.

The post ends there. There's nothing further about the
meeting. This post is far more troubling and revealing
than the previous ones. It shows matters coming to a
head between the local community and the mining
companies. But who is this man 'Tonio' that Christina
refers to? I need to find out. That meeting was crucial.
It may have been what killed her.

Chapter 21: Hennessy

Rupert Hennessy's phone rang. He didn't give his number out freely so a call from a private number was unusual.

"Am I speaking to Rupert Hennessy from *Free People News*?" It was a woman's voice he didn't recognise.

"Who is this?"

"I'd prefer not to give my name at this point. I have important information about the Green Shoots case."

"I'm listening."

"I would prefer not to talk over the phone, as it may not be secure. Would it be possible to meet?"

"You need to do better than that. My time is precious. How do I know you're not wasting it?"

"I'm a private investigator, working for the family of one of the victims. I have discovered links between the killings and a certain protest group. I have evidence."

"I assume you're talking about XR. Do you have specific names?"

"Not over the phone, but one of them is a prominent

activist who was arrested in a riot recently, then expelled."

Hennessy noted 'Jackson' down on his pad.

"I also have evidence that the people behind the killings have been in contact with a former colleague of yours – John Adamson. He may also be involved."

Hennessy made another note. That would be gold dust if true. He should pursue it.

"I will be sat at the back of the Blind Beggar in Whitechapel at midday. I will wait ten minutes only. Blonde hair, black jacket."

Before Hennessy could reply, she hung up. Something about the call seemed off, but his reporter's instinct took over. He looked at his watch. He had nearly an hour to get to the East End, so it was easily done. He put his jacket on and headed out of the office.

The Blind Beggar was getting busy as the lunchtime crowd started to build. Hennessy remembered now why the pub sounded familiar – the Blind Beggar was a Krays pub back in the sixties. These days it was more London office workers than gangsters, but he still felt out of place. His haunts were more West End than East End, more private clubs and wine bars than pubs.

He made his way to the back of the pub but couldn't see her. Just as he was beginning to wonder if it was a prank, a woman brushed past him and said in a low voice, "Take a seat, Mr Hennessy." They sat opposite each other in an alcove, obscured from the rest of the pub. She fixed him with a stare. She was strikingly attractive.

She took an envelope from her jacket. Taking out a large print, she placed it on the table. Hennessy leaned forward and saw a man handing a leaflet to another. He looked closer. It was Abel Jackson and the other man looked familiar.

"Keith Blakely, the first Green Shoots victim."

She produced another photograph. This time it showed Jackson with another man. Hennessy said, "The second victim, Jeremy Grover, isn't it? Have you taken these to the police?"

"Not yet. Why give something away when it's clearly of value?"

Hennessy nodded and smiled. So this was about money.

"You also mentioned John Adamson?"

"Yes. I have much more than this, footage as well as stills. I will show you a clip on my laptop, but outside, not in here, and no more than that until we've discussed the information's value."

She got up and made for the rear exit. Glancing over her shoulder, she said curtly, "Now or never, Mr Hennessy."

Hennessy hesitated before following her into an alleyway. As his sense of unease began to return, she took out a laptop from a bag and placed it on the bonnet of a car. She tapped a few keys and invited him to look. She stepped aside and Hennessy bent over the laptop. There was a grainy image he couldn't make out. He clicked to enlarge it.

"We don't have much time," she said.

Hennessy looked at the video, which showed a man leaning over a car. Just as he was puzzling over this, she added, "Or rather, you don't have much time."

He saw a shape appear on screen behind the man and just as his eyes widened in realisation, he felt something clamped over his mouth and nose. There was a strong chemical smell. His legs buckled as he lost consciousness.

***

Rupert Hennessy woke up with a throbbing headache. He was lying on a table. He tried to move but something restricted him. He raised his head a few inches to see his legs were bound together and he was tied down to the table.

"Mr Hennessy, nice of you to join me."

He saw a man in a black balaclava looking down at him. He could see from his mouth that the man was smiling, baring his teeth. He couldn't see the woman.

Hennessy's mouth was dry, his nostrils still full of what he assumed was chloroform. "What is this? Who are you?"

The man chuckled. "Oh, Rupert. I would have expected better questions from a journalist. Have a think. I'm sure you know."

Hennessy looked at him and winced as his head

pounded.

"I'm sorry about my method of setting up our little *tête à tête*. But what can you expect from… how did you put it again? Oh yes, a 'sick anarchist with a twisted cause'?"

Hennessy knew now who he was and began to panic, straining his arms and pushing with his legs, but it was futile. He was held fast.

"Oh, don't bother struggling and don't worry either, Rupert. I do intend to let you go. That's why I'm wearing this, you see." He gestured to the mask. "Were we having this meeting face to face as it were, it wouldn't bode well for your future. Not at all. So take comfort in that and relax. You'll get off this table when I let you."

The man then placed a clamp over Hennessy's nose so that he had to breathe through his mouth.

"What are you doing?"

"I'm just going to ask you some questions. I advise you to choose your answers carefully. Are you ready?"

Rupert stared at him, noting the features he could see: dark eyes, he was white, teeth in good condition, tall and muscular. The man was smiling again. He seemed to be enjoying this.

"First question: do you believe that climate change is a hoax, yes or no?"

Hennessy looked at the ceiling, searching for the right answer.

"Come on now, it's a simple question. Yes or no?"

"No."

The man lifted a container and poured green liquid into Hennessy's mouth. Hennessy closed his mouth instinctively but eventually he had to breathe and opened it, his mouth filling with liquid. He coughed and heaved.

The man stopped pouring. "That's what you get for lying, Rupert. You called it the 'climate change hoax' in a recent article, yet you don't believe it?"

Hennessy was breathing heavily. "Not a hoax, maybe exaggerated, I don't know!"

"You don't know? So you write about things you don't even understand?"

Hennessy said nothing.

"Next question. Do you think the oil industry is doing great work in renewable technology?"

Hennessy hesitated and decided to give his real opinion this time. "Yes, I do."

"And you believe this outweighs the harm they do in producing fossil fuels?"

"I… I don't know. Maybe."

The man poured. Hennessy choked.

"Maybe is not a choice, Rupert. Yes or no?"

"No!"

"Do you know what we call it when a polluting company makes a big show about caring for the Earth, Rupert?"

Hennessy was coughing, his answer indecipherable.

"No idea? We call it 'greenwash', Rupert. You see

this is what we're doing here now. I'm greenwashing you!"

The man laughed and carried on pouring. This time, Hennessy moved his head sharply to the side to evade the liquid.

"Another question. Do you believe that peaceful protesters are terrorists?"

"No."

He poured more liquid. "Then why did you write that in your article? Do you think they are as bad as... well, the likes of me?"

Hennessy heaved and spat. "No! I write that because that's what readers want!"

"So you write lies, knowing they are lies?"

Hennessy looked directly into the dark eyes. He knew there was no point lying.

"All journalists do. It gets people reading. You have to understand!"

"Oh, I understand. You and others like you lie to poison people's minds. Do you admit it?"

Hennessy felt he had no choice. "Yes." He spluttered and gasped for air. He was nauseous from swallowing so much liquid. His head and upper body were now covered in paint, his white shirt splattered green.

"I think that's enough. You've done quite well, Rupert."

Hennessy turned his head and vomited onto the floor. Slowly his breathing began to return to normal.

"I won't say anything about this. I'll even write what

you want me to write. Just let me go. You said as I haven't seen your face…"

"Yes, yes. Soon, Rupert, but first I have something to give you."

He took hold of Hennessy's arm and produced a needle. Hennessy struggled.

The man's smile disappeared. "Hold still or I'll stick this in your neck instead."

He injected Hennessy in the arm. Hennessy stopped struggling and lay still, expecting to pass out, but nothing happened.

The man held up a photograph. Hennessy squinted at it. It was a brown snake with a flattened head and yellow zig-zag pattern down its body.

"This is the fer-de-lance viper, which, as I'm sure a man of your education knows, means 'spear of fire' in French. It is one of the most venomous and aggressive snakes in Latin America. I prefer to call it by the name locals give it though, as I feel it's more appropriate: '*el equis*' – 'the X'.

"It proved too difficult to get the snake itself, but I got hold of some venom. It didn't come cheap either, Rupert. I've spent quite a lot of money on this – on you."

Rupert's eyes widened and he looked at his arm.

"You may have noticed from the circumstances of the other victims that I am fond of, shall we say, poetic justice. In this case, poison is repaid with poison. You are quite a venomous snake yourself, so I'm sure you appreciate the irony, Rupert."

Rupert thrashed around at the ropes. "I was right, you are sick!"

"I'd choose your words more carefully, Rupert. I could always just leave you on this table to die if you'd prefer?"

Hennessy was silent again.

"Now, as you did so well earlier, I've decided to play fair. I have injected you with enough poison to be fatal in about an hour but I didn't inject into a vein so you may have longer than that. That's the exciting part! We are close to a hospital here so you have time to alert doctors and obtain the anti-venom. I already checked and they do have it in London.

"Listen carefully. I'm going to cut the ropes around your arms in a moment. You should have no trouble in untying the ropes around your legs. I will leave the door open. When you get outside, there is an alleyway. Walk to the right up the alley and you will be on Whitechapel Road. A ten-minute walk to the right is the Royal London Hospital. I would advise you not to run as that will increase the blood flow and quicken the spread of the poison. Show the doctors this photograph of the fer-de-lance. They can obtain the anti-venom and neutralise the poison inside you. Then your rehabilitation will be complete. Goodbye, Rupert."

The man cut the ropes around Hennessy's arms. When he was sure he was gone, Hennessy lifted himself up and, seeing a penknife on the table between his legs, he reached for it and began cutting the other ropes.

He got off the table but immediately slipped barefoot on the paint soaking the concrete floor, banging his head as he fell. He was covered in green paint and groggy. He couldn't find his shoes, so he stumbled barefoot towards an unbolted metal door and into the alleyway.

To his right, he heard the distant sound of sirens and traffic rumbling past. He started to jog up the alleyway, then remembered he needed to keep his heart rate down. He slowed to an ambling walk, the ground hurting his bare feet, and he soon came out onto a main road.

He looked to the right and could see the modern buildings of the Royal London Hospital looming over the road like a giant blue and grey Rubik's cube. He thought of calling an ambulance but he was so close to the hospital there would be no point, and his phone was gone anyway.

He tried to flag down a taxi but none stopped. Drivers looked at him in horror and pedestrians stopped in shock and amusement at the sight of a dishevelled man covered in green paint, stumbling barefoot down the road.

Hennessy reached the Accident and Emergency department of the hospital, made his way through the entrance and collapsed on the floor, vomiting. Two nurses rushed towards him. His vision was becoming blurred. He reached in his pocket for the photograph and whispered through laboured breathing, "Poison... fer-de-lance snake... need anti-venom." The nurse held up the photo and looked at her colleague in confusion.

"I'm sorry, are you saying you've been bitten by a snake?"

Hennessy's speech became slurred. "Injection... attempted murder... anti-venom." He tried to pat his upper arm.

Two paramedics lifted Hennessy onto a hospital trolley and wheeled him through to the emergency room, where the nurses informed the duty doctor. Doctor Patel studied the photograph and examined the needle mark in Hennessy's arm before putting in a call to nearby Guy's Hospital. After explaining the emergency, the consultant at Guy's ordered a vial of anti-venom to be sent over by ambulance.

Dr Patel returned to examine Hennessy, who by now was barely conscious. Dr Patel frowned. If this were fer-de-lance venom, there would be haemotoxic symptoms – extreme pain, swelling and tissue damage around the injection – but there were none. He checked Hennessy's oxygen levels. His breathing was becoming shallow and oxygen levels falling. They needed to get him on a ventilator as soon as possible.

Dr Patel called the nurses and they wheeled in a ventilator. Suddenly, Hennessy's torso went into spasm, shaking uncontrollably as the nurses tried to connect the ventilator. Hennessy's body stopped shaking and was still. Dr Patel checked for a pulse and began resuscitation. He continued for ten minutes, but Rupert Hennessy was dead.

Dr Patel recorded the time of death. He could never

get used to losing a patient, and particularly one so young. His driver's licence showed he was just twenty-five. Dr Patel looked again at the photograph of the snake. The anti-venom had not arrived in time but even so, he'd seen haemotoxic snake bites in the tropics and the symptoms simply didn't fit. It didn't make sense. He turned over the photograph. Written on the other side in green ink was one word: 'LIES'.

Chapter 22

I'll be the first to admit I never really liked him, but nobody deserves to die like that. It looks like Rupert Hennessy was not only poisoned but tortured as well.

A pedestrian took a photo of him covered in green paint stumbling along the road to the hospital. It's on the front page of several news sites: 'Minutes from death: journalist's agonising final journey'.

In contrast to Liu's death, I'm not nearly the first on the scene. The police and reporters are already at the hospital when I make it to Whitechapel in the evening.

I talk to the doctors, who confirm paint was found in Hennessy's stomach and lungs, but this was not the cause of death. They detected a neurotoxin likely to be from a snake of the cobra family such as the coral snake. It seems the killers deliberately misinformed Hennessy by giving him a photo of a different snake with a totally different class of venom.

Things become quite awkward when a fellow hack remembers I worked with Hennessy and asks me for a quote paying tribute to him. I find it hard to come up with the right words but I manage to say he was talented, hard-working and died far too young, all of which was true.

I don't stay long at the hospital as the news desk already has most of the facts, so I head home to try to clear my head.

Steve has texted me: 'Heard about Rupert. This is out of control. Are you okay?'

I'm not okay. I feel physically sick. It's not just the way he died but the fact that the killers targeted a journalist. It makes me wonder even more about my own safety. How can I write honestly about what is going on, particularly as I'm being followed? I might be next if these people don't like what I write.

I get on a train home. Opposite me is a young couple wrapped in each other's arms – the last thing I want to see. There's nowhere else to sit so I just put up with it.

Sometimes I just hate everyone, especially lovers. I want to tell them, don't you know one day this will all end? One of you will eventually lose the other. You'd better hope you stop loving each other long before that happens.

They see me watching them and smile knowingly at each other, as if to say, 'don't mind him, he doesn't understand'. But I understand only too well. I was like you once, and now I ride this train alone with an empty seat next to me, where once there was the most wonderful woman I'd ever met.

At times like this when I hate the world and everyone

in it, I wonder if that's what leads people to do unspeakable things. If there's no life worth living, then the only perverse pleasure left would be to take the happiness from other people.

I wonder if that's Root's story. When all else fails, kill them all. I can't imagine it would feel better though. I'm not a violent man either. I'd rather die than take another human life, but then what do I do with all this hatred?

It's a relief to get home. I know I should do some more work on Christina's research and read through her blog again to see if I've missed anything, but I just don't have the energy. I notice I tire very quickly when I'm working on it – the stress and emotion it stirs up is exhausting.

I have a shot of brandy and try to get some shut-eye but I only sleep in fits and starts. There are too many people haunting my dreams now. Not only Christina but Liu choking on meat and now Rupert Hennessy covered in paint, wide-eyed and delirious. He's calling out at me, saying it's my fault what happened to him.

I'm woken from restless half sleep by banging at the door. It takes me a while to register if I'm still dreaming. Police. Did I hear that right? I sit up.

"Mr Adamson, open the door. It's the police."

What the hell? I glance at the clock. It's six a.m. I get out of bed and walk to the door.

"What do you want?"

"It's DCI Morrison. Open the door now, please."

I'm hardly going to stop the police coming in. I open the door and have to immediately step aside as two officers burst into the flat past me.

A man I don't recognise steps forward. "John Adamson, I'm Mike Edmunds from Counter Terrorism. We need to bring you in to answer some questions on the Green Shoots case."

He's short, stocky and bald. He fixes me with a glare. He clearly means business.

"You're not kidding, are you? Am I under arrest?"

DCI Morrison interjects. "We're hoping that won't be necessary, John. It would be better if you come in voluntarily and answer some questions. We have reason to believe you have information that can assist the investigation."

I walk back towards the bedroom and see an officer carrying my laptop.

"Hey, what are you doing with that?"

Edmunds enters the flat. "Mr Adamson, can you confirm this is your work laptop where you keep your journalism work and email accounts?"

"Yes but…"

"Then we will need to analyse its contents as part of our enquiries."

I look at DCI Morrison, who nods. I could insist they bring a warrant but with Counter Terrorism, it's not the best idea. I have nothing to hide from them anyway.

I get dressed and go down to a police car. No cuffs. I remind myself I'm just helping them with enquiries. We drive into London through Streatham, Tooting then Vauxhall. We must be going to Scotland Yard. I've been there enough times, but never to be questioned.

We drive up a side street to a back entrance, which is a relief because there's a camp of press at the front of the Yard. An officer takes my details, then asks me to empty my pockets. He takes my wallet, keys and phone.

"Is this really necessary?"

"Just procedural. You should get it all back soon enough."

I'm led into an interview room and left alone. Steve was right. I should have gone to the police earlier with what I know, but I was too focused on getting more information about Christina.

I wonder what they're doing with my laptop. I've backed up my research on both the Green Shoots case and Christina's case, so I'm not too concerned about losing any information, but it's a blatant intrusion.

The door opens and in comes Edmunds followed by Morrison.

"I brought you tea, John. Milk. I couldn't remember if you took sugar." She sets the cup and sachets down on the table.

"Thanks. If you wanted me to come in, why the dawn patrol and why take my laptop?"

"Mike Edmunds here is from Counter Terrorism, John. I'm afraid we don't have time to stand on ceremony." I get the feeling that's Morrison's way of telling me this raid was his idea, not hers.

Edmunds clears his throat. "No, we don't have time. Mr Adamson, I could do this more formally and hold you for several days under the Counter Terrorism Act but I hope that won't be necessary. We've got five deaths now, four of which are in our jurisdiction, and nobody thinks it will stop there. I'll be honest, I don't like journalists. You're all about making a splash and chasing readers, but DCI Morrison speaks highly of you and I'm taking that into account. I understand you've won a few awards for work leading to the arrest of criminals. Brilliant. For me that's called doing my job. I don't get awards."

He pauses and looks at me. "Tell me about your dealings with Rupert Hennessy."

This takes me by surprise. I'd expected them to ask about Root and his tip-offs.

"I worked with Rupert for a year or so. He was very... ambitious."

"Ambitious? Not 'insufferable and arrogant'?" Edmunds is reading from his notebook. "At least that's what colleagues said you thought of him. It was well-known the two of you didn't get on. He even mentioned it in his exit interview, I'm told."

"Did he? I'm not sure what you're getting at here. Rupert and I didn't exactly get on, but he was talented and what happened yesterday was appalling."

"Yes, it was. While we're on the subject, where were you yesterday afternoon between midday and six p.m.?"

"Good grief. Am I a suspect? This is ridiculous!"

"Answer the question."

"I was at home. I left when the news desk informed me of the killing. It would have been around six p.m. when I went to the hospital."

"Can anyone confirm you were at home prior to that?"

"No, I live alone. Why are you asking this? You should be going after the people who did this, not a reporter!"

Edmunds raises his eyebrows and makes a note. "I'm asking because we recovered Rupert Hennessy's notebook from his pocket. As you can see from this photograph, it is stained with the same green paint he was tortured with. I wonder if you could read the last words he wrote in it?"

Edmunds lays the photo on the table and pushes it towards me. It reads simply: "John Adamson?"

"Now can you see why we're so keen to know your whereabouts?"

If Edmunds' intention is to shock me into silence, he's succeeded.

I think about it for a moment. "I can only guess that Rupert wondered why I was so quick off the mark in reporting the killings. Knowing him, it would have irritated him that a rival was getting information before him."

Edmunds snorts. "We'll come back to where you're getting information later. Can you confirm where you were the afternoon and evening of 10th March?"

10th March – the day Liu was killed.

"I was at home alone."

"Can anyone confirm that?"

"No."

"I see. And what about the morning of 11th March?"

"I received a tip-off about Mr Liu and went to Romilly Street."

"Did you arrive before the police?"

I hesitate for a moment. "I think we arrived at almost exactly the same time."

"Are you sure about that Mr Adamson?"

"Possibly a few moments before the police."

"A few moments before. So that would explain this then?"

Edmunds produces another photo. It's me crouching next to Liu's body.

"You see we also receive anonymous tip-offs, Mr Adamson."

Who on earth took this photo and how did the police get it?

"I was there literally a couple of minutes before the police arrived. I introduced myself to the officers and then waited outside."

"But how exactly did you know there would be a body at that address?"

"I received an email. A photograph of the body and the address."

"It didn't occur to you to inform the police of this? It didn't occur to you that it might be the killers themselves sending you this?"

"Yes, it did, but…"

"But the story was the priority?"

Difficult to argue with that.

"Let's come back to your tip-offs. Where were you during the afternoon and evening of 28th February?"

"At home alone. And no, nobody can confirm that."

"And 19th February?"

"The same. You could check the CCTV outside my building, perhaps? I was inside for weeks on end. I bought groceries online. There's only one exit from the building."

Edmunds snorts again. "You can see our problem, Mr Adamson. You know a lot about these killings, sometimes more than the police, and you have no alibi for any of them."

I begin to lose my temper. "Look, I don't know if you are aware that my wife died recently. I have spent most of the past five months grieving at home. That's what people do. I scarcely left the flat in months and in the past few weeks most of my outings have been to follow up on this case. You can't seriously believe I'm going around London killing businessmen?"

"It's not about what I believe, Mr Adamson. The facts show that you are somehow involved. I am trying to ascertain to what extent."

There's a knock at the door and Edmunds goes outside to talk with an officer.

Morrison, who has sat listening silently until now,

leans forward and says in a low voice, "John, Edmunds is currently keeping an open mind, so you need to tell him everything you know about where you've been getting your information. It's in everybody's best interests."

Edmunds comes back carrying my laptop and places it in front of me.

"Right, Mr Adamson. We can see that you have photographs of all five crime scenes. We've compared them with police photographs and they are not official crime scene images. They must have been taken before the police arrived. Can you tell me how you came to be in possession of these?"

"The first set of photographs of Keith Blakely was sent to *The Sentinel* on a USB, then biked over to me."

"Do you have this USB?"

"No. I downloaded the photos and sent it back to the office. My colleague Steve Hartley may know where the USB is, and he can confirm that is exactly what happened."

"Your close friend Steve Hartley? Hmm. We will need to recover that USB. It could well be evidence. What about the photos from the other killings?"

"They were all emailed to me from different addresses each time, always with the name 'Root' in the address. Do you want me to show you?"

Edmunds nods. I take the laptop, open up my email and find the folder where I have saved all information on the Green Shoots case, including all emails. I pass

Edmunds the laptop.

He scrolls through them, frowning. "We'll need to access all these emails and trace the senders. Apart from the USB and emails, have you had any other communication with this source?"

I hesitate. I'd hoped to avoid this conversation.

Edmunds notices immediately. "I'd say you have then."

He places my phone on the table. He already knows.

"There have been a couple of phone calls and texts, always from a private number."

"Show me."

I scroll through my texts and show him the text I received after the press conference, and then the text from Beachy Head.

Edmunds reads aloud: "'Don't do it, John. Turn off the engine'. Don't do what?"

Not for the first time, I can't find the words.

Edmunds looks at the message again. "What exactly were you doing or about to do at two a.m. on 26th February?"

There's no point in lying. "I was in my car at Beachy Head."

"Okay, Mr Adamson. We already know that. The officers who detained you filed a report, even though you weren't charged. Procedural. They were concerned for your safety, according to the report. You were breathalysed and released without charge. That must have been a relief."

"Like I said, grief can be overwhelming. I was in a bad way that night."

"Yes clearly, and I'm sorry for your loss. As you say, grief can do terrible things, and it can make people do terrible things too. But how did this person know where you were?"

"I don't know, but as you can see from the text after the press conference, he appears to be following me."

"You mentioned phone calls, so you have actually talked to him?"

"Once, yes. He called me the day after I was on Beachy Head. He gave his name as 'Root', unlikely to be his real name of course, but it must be the same person who sent the emails."

"What did he say on the phone?"

I really don't want to get into this but it seems I have no choice.

"He told me he had reason to believe that something else happened to my wife in South America. I'd been told she died of a tropical disease but he implied he had evidence and wanted me to look into Blakely's death. He said it was a 'quid pro quo' situation."

"Quid pro quo? I see. Do you think there is any truth in his claims about your wife?"

"Yes, I do, in fact. I have uncovered threats against her shortly before her death. I think he may be right but it's not an easy investigation, particularly given that it happened on the other side of the world."

"Do you think there is some connection then between

what happened to your wife and the Green Shoots killings?"

"I honestly don't know."

I know exactly what he's going to do next. In fact, he already has it prepared. He picks up his phone and brings up the still of Christina from the video.

"Can you confirm this woman is your late wife, Mr Adamson?"

"Yes."

"You know where it's taken from, I presume?"

I nod.

"So you can see why we wonder at your involvement. We have murders justified by the perpetrators as revenge for the deaths of eco-activists, one of whom was your late wife. I'd say that's a big coincidence and provides a strong motive, wouldn't you?"

I lose my temper and bang the desk. "This is insane. I don't kill people! I report. I investigate. It's not a coincidence at all. This sicko deliberately put that photo of my wife on that video as a message to me. He's played me like a bloody violin reporting on these crimes. In return, he keeps drip feeding me information about my wife."

I'm standing up, jabbing my finger at Edmunds. When I finish shouting, he looks at me for a long time. "So now we're getting to it. Sit down please, Mr Adamson. So, you report on the killings and he feeds you information on your wife's death. Is that all?"

I sit down. Shouting at a counter-terrorism agent isn't my finest hour. I try to calm down. "Yes, I think he basically wanted me to break the story and generate media coverage."

"You certainly did that. He did 'play you like a bloody violin', didn't he?"

"Look, I've told you all I know. That's all I have on my laptop there. I want you to catch these people, but I didn't bring all this to the police because I'm trying to find out what happened to my wife and I'm sure this man knows more. That's the only reason. I was worried he would stop giving me information if I went to the police, but given that he's following me and after what happened to Rupert, I don't exactly feel safe."

"If you are being followed then we can presume this man knows by now you've been interviewed by the police, but has he actually threatened you? From what you've said, he's traded favours and supplied information on your wife's death, so it's a relationship of convenience."

"Yes, but I'm not much use to him now that it's a huge story. He doesn't need me anymore."

"Perhaps not. Okay, Mr Adamson, we're going to make sure we've got everything off your laptop that may be of use, then you will be free to go. We'll be keeping a close eye on you, although I don't think police protection is appropriate at this point."

Somehow, I don't think protecting me figures on his priority list at all.

Edmunds gets up. "If this man or any of his associates get in touch, I expect you to notify us immediately, is that clear? Some of my colleagues think your actions in this case could amount to interfering in a police enquiry. I'm not sure I agree... for now."

Edmunds glares at me to ensure this has sunk in and they both leave. I wait in the interview room until an officer finally comes through and escorts me out, giving me back my laptop, phone, keys and wallet. I leave Scotland Yard through the same back door.

It's ten a.m. I've been here for hours. For a moment, I wonder if that all actually happened. It feels surreal, but then everything does about this case.

There are so many unanswered questions: why was my name the last thing Hennessy wrote down? And who took that photo of me at the Liu crime scene? I've been thinking about the angle of the shot. There was a skylight in that room. I had wondered if I saw someone out there. They must have been out on the roof with a camera. It could have been the killer, just metres away from me.

I'm exhausted, so I hail a cab to get home quickly. The Hennessy story is on the radio. I ask the driver to turn it up. There are some new details. Hennessy was last seen at the Blind Beggar pub in Whitechapel. The reporter mentions that it's the pub made notorious when Ronnie Kray shot George Cornell there in the 1960s. That can't be a coincidence – it's got Root's black humour written all over it. There are witness reports of

Hennessy talking to a woman with blonde hair in the pub. Another woman, but different hair colour this time. He definitely has an accomplice then, or several.

I get back to the flat and collapse on the bed. The Green Shoots case has been taking over my life. I need to get some control back rather than constantly reacting to what's happening. More importantly, I need to make more progress on Christina. I've scoured all the posts on her blog and I don't think there's anything else that will help.

I don't know if I'm in danger in London, but I need to get out. If I'm honest with myself, I've known for a while that to really find out what happened to Christina, I don't just need to get out of London. I need to go to Ecuador.

Chapter 23: Jackson

Abel Jackson jabbed at his computer keyboard, shifting in his chair. He got up and walked around the room, then sat down again. At first, it had been exciting when someone from an anti-capitalist group contacted him to do some work 'off the books' a few weeks ago. He was told it was strictly confidential and not to talk to anyone.

A bit of hacking, a bit of people watching, some handing out leaflets – most of the work was easy and Jackson had wondered why the pay was so high. He wasn't complaining though, and he'd even got a new laptop out of it. These people must be well-funded.

Then they asked him to cause some trouble at the protest, which he was only happy to do. He'd become a bit of a folk hero too because of that, so it was all good.

When they sent him a script a couple of weeks ago and instructed him to send an audio file, he didn't think twice, especially when he saw the payment. But when the video was released with his voice on it, he grew scared of what he'd got involved in, even though it was kind of exhilarating. He reminded himself that the voice disguise was there to protect him and it was unlikely anyone would know it was him.

Jackson hadn't heard from his source for a while until he received a simple text message: 'Urgent instructions to follow. Stand by'.

He kept nervously checking his email account, then a message came in.

Dear Mr Jackson,

For your own protection, please find attached a script. Record an MP4 video and send it via file transfer.

Please also note a delivery is en route. Open the white package immediately. Turn on the silver phone and wait for our call.

The brown package is for emergency use only. Do NOT open until instructed.

A further transfer has been sent with thanks.

"For my own protection?" He didn't like the sound of that.

He read through the script – denial of involvement, claims of police corruption, a call to action and a rousing quote at the end. After thinking through his options, he decided it was a good idea. Although it wasn't clear if the police would actually press ahead with charges, it looked like the authorities were hell-bent on striking back hard.

He recorded the video, taking a few times to get the script right and saying it with the right tone and feeling.

It felt strange to watch himself back.

He sent the video and waited. He then checked his bank account and his jaw dropped when he saw the size of the transfer. He could take the rest of the year off with that payment.

His buzzer sounded. He picked up but there was no answer. He opened the door to see the packages already on the doormat. He looked around but saw nobody. Whoever delivered it must have buzzed on their way out. Jackson opened the white package and found four phones inside. He picked up the silver one and turned it on.

***

DCI Morrison moved away from the computer so that DS Harman and agent Edmunds could view the images. Edmunds sucked air through his teeth as he looked at each of them. "Definitely a match on all three. So, we've got contact with three victims – Blakely, Grover and Liu – on the days they disappeared. That's more than enough to make an arrest. But combined with this new evidence..."

Harman interjected. "What new evidence?"

Edmunds continued. "The voice distorter used on the video was pretty crude. I asked the tech team to take a close look at it and they've managed to unscramble the audio. We can't be a hundred per cent sure, but comparing it with his voice from the protest, we're reasonably sure it's a match. It wouldn't necessarily stand up in court but I say we bring him in."

There was a knock at the door. It was a sergeant from DCI Morrison's team.

"Sorry to interrupt but there's been an urgent development. A victim's phone just turned on. We've pinpointed the location."

He passed a piece of paper to DCI Morrison, who showed it to Harman and Edmunds.

Edmunds turned to his colleagues. "We've got him. Send a unit there now."

***

Abel Jackson sat on the couch, staring at the phone. He was sweating, trying to think of his next move. He realised he couldn't trust these people. Now they'd given him these phones, he wondered what else they wanted him to do.

He felt a strong urge to get out of his flat and run. He looked in the drawer for his passport. With this latest payment he could fly anywhere. Somewhere remote. He thought of the Himalayas he'd visited last year. That would work. They'd never find him there and it was a beautiful place. He started to look on his phone for flights but then thought it would be better to go straight to the airport and get on the first flight. He reached for his jacket.

The silver phone rang. Jackson wanted to ignore it

and throw it away, but these people could be dangerous. Better to let them think he was following their instructions. Meantime, he could leave before they even realised.

"Mr Jackson, listen carefully."

Jackson didn't recognise the man's voice.

"We have been compromised. *You* have been compromised. Do not attempt to leave the country as they will be watching airports and ports."

Jackson froze. How did this guy know what he was planning already? He needed a plan B then.

"Okay. What do I do?"

Jackson heard bangs and shouts on the line.

"It's too late. They're here. They're nearly at your door. There's no time. Mr Jackson, they are *not* police. Open the brown package. Resist!" The line cut off.

If they're not police, then who is coming? Maybe he still had time to get out. Jackson opened the curtains a crack and looked down at the street. It was quiet. He couldn't see anyone except a couple walking their dog.

Jackson got a bag, unplugged the laptop and packed it along with a change of clothes. He could go out the fire escape. As he moved towards the door, he heard a loud bang followed by heavy thuds. They were already coming up the stairs. He'd run out of time. He moved back from the door.

He couldn't think. He shook his head to get a grip. He looked back at the brown envelope on the couch. Scrawled across the back of the jiffy bag in green marker was 'Emergency use only'. He picked it up and opened it. There was a black object inside bubble wrap.

Jackson heard more thuds outside and saw shadows blocking the light underneath the door. They were standing either side of it.

"Abel Jackson. Armed police. Open the door."

The man on the phone said they were not police. Jackson fixed his eyes on the door then looked again at the package. It was wrapped tightly. He used his teeth to tear it open. He moved to the corner away from the door. The man said he should resist, but there were too many of them.

The door exploded open just as Jackson tore off the package to reveal a pistol. Two armed policemen pointed their rifles at him.

"Hands up! Drop the weapon!"

The two commands came together. Something in Jackson's brain made him obey the first command and he started to raise his hands. An officer instinctively pulled the trigger as Jackson raised the pistol. Two shots to the chest sent him hurtling back into the corner.

He squeezed the trigger as he fell. A ball of green paint splattered the opposite wall. Jackson squinted at the pistol, which fell from his hand. His last thought was that someone had screwed him. His eyes glazed over as his heart stopped beating.

Chapter 24

I've spent the past hour browsing websites for flights to Ecuador. I haven't decided when to go yet. I should clear it with the editor and wait for things to calm down on this case before leaving.

I need to go soon though, otherwise I'll go crazy. It already feels so long since I started investigating what happened to Christina, but it's little more than a month. I've really lost track of time.

My phone rings. It's Matt, the deputy news editor.

"John, have you seen about Hackney?"

"No, I've been head down in research."

"The police shot a man dead resisting arrest. A suspect in the Green Shoots case, according to the Met. Can you get down there? We're expecting a statement."

They've got him already? I'm a bit embarrassed to be caught off guard by the news desk, but a quick scan of news sites shows it's only just broken. The raid happened less than an hour ago. There are very few details, but the dead man is Abel Jackson. The dreadlocked eco-warrior who sprayed a racist with paint is a suspect in the Green Shoots killings? That's a shock, but anything is possible.

I head into London and get to the address – a drab, grey block of flats. There's a cluster of police vans, a media pack and crowd of bystanders. Most of the usual media suspects are already here. For many journalists, the Green Shoots case is the chance of a lifetime. I find myself instinctively looking around for Rupert, then shake the thought from my head. Jackson was even younger than him.

A middle-aged black woman is shouting at the police and being pulled back. I move closer to hear her. "He never did harm to nobody. You murderers!"

Jim from *The Times* whispers to me, "That's his mother."

Her companion starts waving journalists away and pushes a cameraman. "Get your camera out of here. She's just lost her son. Don't you have any humanity?"

Intruding on someone's grief has always been the most uncomfortable part of reporting crime for me. I used to hate doing 'death knocks' to ask relatives for their reaction to the death of a loved one. I've had more than enough doors slammed in my face and insults hurled at me. It feels too much like vultures picking over bones, but editors want those quotes. I couldn't imagine being on the receiving end of that kind of attention, having cameras jammed in my face after Christina died. It would be hell. I'd probably lash out too.

Jackson's mother is escorted away by relatives.

There's still a crowd milling around. More officers arrive in vans. It seems unnecessary but the police must be concerned about trouble kicking off.

I get a call from the news desk. There will be a statement at Scotland Yard at midday. That's in half an hour. I'm not surprised the police are talking to the media over there because the situation here is very tense. Many of the crowd are on the move too. They must have heard about the press conference.

Jim and a group of journalists offer to share a taxi. Jim thinks the trouble will get worse. "There's a rumour Jackson had a paintball gun when they shot him dead. I don't know how the police are going to handle it but people in this neighbourhood will take a lot of calming down."

We get over to the Yard and at midday a group of senior officers emerge. No assistant chief constable this time; it's Edmunds, the agent who interviewed me. Morrison is with him too. She looks a bit shaken, while Edmunds looks grimly determined. We make eye contact briefly. I want to show him I have nothing to be ashamed of.

Edmunds begins. "This morning, after receiving intelligence in connection with the Green Shoots investigation, armed police were dispatched to make an arrest at the residence of Mr Abel Jackson in Hackney. Armed officers made their presence known but Mr Jackson did not answer the door. On entering the flat, officers saw Mr Jackson in possession of what appeared to be a firearm. The suspect ignored orders to drop the weapon. He was shot and pronounced dead at the scene."

"Lying scum!" a man shouts from behind me.

Edmunds ignores the interruption and continues. "Officers examined Mr Jackson's firearm and found it to be a pellet gun. The death of the suspect is tragic and regrettable, but we are confident that protocol was followed."

"Bullshit!"

It's getting rowdy and the crowd is angry. They certainly got here fast.

Edmunds continues but struggles to be heard above the shouting. "Officers searched the premises and found substantial evidence linking Mr Jackson to the victims of the Green Shoots killings. We are continuing our investigation and we urge members of the public to come forward with information, particularly those who knew Mr Jackson. Thank you for your time."

Edmunds abruptly turns and leaves. I'd expected him to take questions, and I think he was planning to do so but changed his mind when confronted with an angry crowd. I want to know more about this 'substantial evidence'.

I'm considering whether to phone the Met to get more details, but then I see my media colleagues glued to their phones. I move forward to see what they're looking at. It's another video, only this time it looks like Jackson. I check my email on my phone and the news

169

desk has forwarded a link. I move away from the crowd to hear it more clearly.

Jackson is looking directly at the camera. It looks like a webcam.

"I've been accused of violence but I am guilty of nothing more than self-defence and legitimate protest against the tyranny of greed. The authorities are trying to take away our right to be heard by labelling us terrorists. They will stop at nothing, even lying and falsifying evidence.

"They will not succeed. We are the future. It's time to choose a side. If you work for these criminal corporations, then quit your job and support our cause. We call on you to reclaim the streets, reclaim the concrete jungle.

"We will not only target the greedy, corrupt destroyers of nature in the streets, but we will hit them where it hurts – in their pockets. Their blood money is not safe from us. We will find it and we will take it and give it to those they have harmed.

"Rise, like lions after slumber, in unvanquishable number. Shake your chains to earth like dew, which in sleep had fallen on you. Ye are many – they are few."

The video ends abruptly. I know those words. It's a quote from Shelley's *Mask of Anarchy*. If London is a tinderbox, a dead man may have just lit the match.

Chapter 25

I'm standing across the street, watching a huge three-storey furniture store burn. Even from this distance, the heat is so searing it burns my eyes and the black smoke is thick with chemicals. I move a block further back but smoke keeps swirling around. It's a windy night so the fire is even more dangerous.

The fire brigade have given up on saving the store itself and are focusing on evacuating the surrounding flats. We thought all the residents had got out but we were wrong. There's a woman screaming from a window. A group of firefighters are below telling her to jump from the second floor. She's crying and coughing. "I can't, I can't!" The fire is spreading fast. She only has seconds to get out.

A firefighter calls out, "I'll catch you. On three, okay?" The woman jerks her head. I can't tell if she's nodding or shaking her head. She finally jumps. Two firefighters catch her and roll to the ground shielding her from impact on the concrete. Seconds later, the window she jumped from erupts in flames.

A bottle smashes behind me. Not everyone has stopped to watch the fire. The looting and rampaging continue. There simply aren't enough police to stop it. I've been covering this most of the day and evening, but this is my cue to leave.

I nearly got stabbed in a riot a few years ago. Christina was appalled and made me promise not to get so close again. I will keep that promise. My life might be a nightmare right now, but I know one thing for sure: I don't want it ending on a Croydon street by a marauding mob.

It's barely half a mile to my flat. I run back. A gang of half a dozen men are coming towards me. I cross the road and one of them starts to cross too, looking to intercept me. "What's your hurry, mate?" I break into a sprint, taking him by surprise. He does a mock ghost impression, raising his arms at me as I run past. I hear them laughing and shouting, but I don't look back or slow down until I'm at the door to my block. I fumble for my keys, breathing hard, and get inside. Safety.

This is the third night in a row of riots, the worst I've seen in London. It started in Hackney with a protest march to the police station, which turned violent when protesters threw missiles at police. Trouble spread to Tottenham and Brixton, then south to the edges of the city and my neck of the woods in Croydon.

Five people are dead, including two police officers, and there have been more than a thousand arrests, not to mention millions of pounds in damage. There was initially some targeting of businesses broadly in line with the Green Shoots targets – petrol stations and banks – but what started as a protest against the police rapidly turned into widespread looting and violence.

I wonder if the Green Shoots killers were aiming for this level of chaos. Knowing Root's black sense of humour, I bet he would approve of the symmetry of burning down a furniture store that likely sold wood from South American forests.

I still find it hard to believe that Jackson was Root, but it looks like he was involved in some way. The police are convinced they got their man. After appeals for calm were ignored, the police released a summary of evidence of Jackson's alleged involvement in the Green Shoots killings. There were CCTV photos of Jackson either handing out leaflets or talking to three of the victims. He had four of the victims' mobile phones in his flat and imagery from all the killings on his computer. There were also several unexplained payments made to him from offshore accounts.

The release of this evidence didn't calm things down at all. In fact, it made things worse. His family accused the police of assassinating their son's character when he could no longer defend himself. In the video, Jackson had predicted 'falsifying' of evidence, so his supporters claimed the police made it up, but I wonder why an innocent man would predict the police planting evidence. And considering how carefully planned the killings were, why would he leave all that evidence in his flat?

If Jackson was involved with the killings, something else doesn't add up to me. I've been searching my memory of that day at the Bank of England. I was standing close to Jackson, but he didn't even give me a second look or appear to recognise me. And unless he was a brilliant voice actor, it definitely wasn't his voice on the phone. Could Jackson have been Root all along? I can't be sure, but I seriously doubt it.

There are clearly accomplices too. Nobody could pull this off alone. Jackson didn't match the description of the suspect in the bar with Blakely, and then there were sightings of women at the deaths of Shawcross and Hennessy.

It's perplexing but if I'm honest with myself, my heart is not in this investigation or in reporting any London crime. I've only seen it as a means to an end to find out what happened to Christina.

I have to go to Ecuador, and soon. I sent a long email to the editor yesterday, recognising the timing was bad. I laid it all out – that I have reason to believe my wife was murdered and I need to go abroad to find out all I can. He was quite understanding. It was not exactly a standard request. To be honest, if he'd said no, I'd probably have resigned and gone anyway.

Steve has come over to my flat. Things have been so crazy in the past week that I haven't even seen him since the police brought me in for questioning. I told him about it over email but tried to downplay it. I knew exactly how he would react.

"I hate to say I told you so, mate. You're under so much stress, it clouded your judgement. No harm done though in the end, hopefully. At least you're not banged up in Wormwood Scrubs!"

I wouldn't last five minutes in a place like that. There would no doubt be criminals I helped the police to convict through my investigative reporting. After what happened to Hennessy though, I'm not sure how safe I am on London streets.

"Listen, John, I'm not sure about this. With the stress you're under, is it really a good idea going across the world? Have you thought through what you can reasonably find out over there?"

"Yes, I'm planning it out. I'm going to start with the hospital to see if I can get anything out of the doctors. Then I'll find the community where Christina stayed. If their leaders were killed, they will want to know what happened as much as I do. Maybe somebody already knows. I also need to find out who this man 'Tonio' is. Christina mentioned him on her blog. He may be involved."

"You haven't mentioned that name before. It sounds like a good plan in theory but let's look at this objectively. Do you really think you'll get anything out of the doctors? They couldn't tell you anything without admitting to malpractice. And as for heading into the jungle with all guns blazing, if the people behind this could have community leaders and Christina killed, do you really think they'd think twice about killing you?"

Steve has a point. I hadn't really thought about my own safety.

"John, I'm not saying it isn't a reasonable plan. I'm just saying it's a lot for someone to do alone."

I've already thought about that, and a local contact would be invaluable. "What about Richie McGill? Do you think I could get him to help out or make some enquiries for me?"

"Way ahead of you, mate. I told him about Christina's case when I contacted him following up on the environmental issues. He said he could help but we'd need to be careful. He's lived out there for years so he knows the lay of the land, and the risks."

"Okay."

"Anyway, I'll cut to the chase, John. It's hard for me to do this environmental report properly from a desk in London. I think I need a field trip. I told the editor it was impossible to get deep into this without witnessing it first-hand."

"Are you talking about coming with me, Steve? Have you discussed it with Alison?"

"Yes. She made me promise to be careful, go with a local guide and get the hell out of there at any sign of trouble."

I don't know what to say. I hadn't even thought of asking Steve to come with me, but this is a lot to take on alone.

The last time I flew to Ecuador was the worst journey of my life. I don't know what I'm getting myself into by returning, but I don't have a choice. It's time to go.

Chapter 26

This is the third time I've flown to Ecuador and the contrast with the first trip could not be greater. It was exciting back then. I took a few months off work and decided to explore South America, a part of the world I'd never visited. I met Christina a month into my trip and an extended holiday became a whirlwind romance that changed my life.

I'm trying to hold on to the memory of that first trip and push away the memories of my last trip in October. As I sit here wide awake on the plane with Steve asleep in the seat next to me, flashes come back of that desperate, hopeless dash across the world.

I try to think about something else. I need to distract myself so I flick through the movies on the in-flight entertainment. I spot a movie we watched together a few years ago. Christina picked it out as she always loved a good romantic movie. It was never my preferred genre but maybe that was because I never really understood romance until I met her. I saw it as something corny and twee for teen pop stars and Hollywood schmaltz –

insincere emotions to tug at the heart strings and pull in the customers.

This particular movie really got to me though. As I watch it again, for a moment I'm back there on the sofa with my arm around Christina, watching an angel who loved a woman so much that he fell from heaven to be with her. Then he lost her and it was unbearable. I remember turning to Christina at the end and saying, "Please don't ever leave me like that." She stroked my arm and told me not to be silly, that she never would.

Christina liked the movie's ending – the fallen angel experiencing the simple joy of bathing in the ocean – but I couldn't get past the devastation of what he'd lost. I remember her saying that the angel had experienced love and now he was experiencing all the world had to offer human beings, so he had hope. I couldn't see that though. All I could see was that he'd lost the love of his life. Now it feels as if I had a premonition. The movie makes me too sad, so I turn it off halfway through. I can't watch that ending again.

***

It's been a few hours since we arrived in Quito. We're sat in a café in the New Town district of Mariscal Sucre, also known as *gringolandia*. Many locals here refer to white foreigners as *gringos*, even though the word originally refers to white Americans.

I haven't been to Mariscal for years but it hasn't

changed much – bars, cafés, hostels and tour operators. There are still a couple of English-style pubs. Richie suggested we stay here because it wouldn't attract much attention to be among so many foreign tourists.

Richie is from California and has been in South America for years, dividing his time mainly between Quito and Bogotá. He seems to know everyone, judging from how many people he greets in the café.

"I got robbed twice in one week when I first arrived here, but I've never been robbed since. I got savvy, and you need to learn fast. Avoid public transport at rush hour and never take an unmarked cab. Don't carry around a lot of cash. Most of it is common sense. Don't let a few thieves make you paranoid though – it's a wonderful city with great people."

Richie is talking so fast he makes my jetlagged head spin, but he's talking more to Steve than me, as it's his first time here. "More of a problem is drawing attention to yourselves. It's dangerous here for journalists to investigate crime. They don't think twice about paying some *matón* from the *Bahía* to have someone whacked. They get away with it too. Even if they're caught, they usually get sprung out of jail pretty fast, so we've got to be careful. You two because you don't know this city well, and me because I live here."

Note to self: try not to get whacked.

Richie asks where I want to start so I tell him about the diagnosis and the doctor at the clinic.

"Clinica Interamericana? That's the most expensive

in the city. It's as close to Western standard care as you'll get here. Most of the rich use it so it's also a money-making machine. I think the owner Paez is close to the current government. We'll have to be careful."

Richie has a car, which makes things easier, and he agrees to drop us off at the hospital. I can't think of a place I want to avoid more than Clinica Interamericana. I've visited it often enough in my nightmares, yet here I am choosing to go back. As we approach the high-rise grey and white building next to the highway, I feel like I can't breathe.

Steve looks over at me. "You okay, John?"

I tell him it's just the altitude. I walk through the entrance. It's not the sight of the hospital that most overwhelms me; it's the smell. It smells exactly the same as that day – a mix of disinfectant and plastic. To most people it would be innocuous, but one sniff and I'm thrown back into hell. I sit down at a row of plastic seats in reception and put my head in my hands. I don't know why I'm putting myself through this.

Steve sits down next to me. "Deep breaths, mate. This won't be easy but you're not doing it alone."

I don't know if I expected it to be easy. I haven't even thought about it. What I'm doing is compulsive. I had to come here.

I need to pull myself together. I get up and ask the receptionist for the office of Dr Javier Gomez, the doctor who told me Christina had died. It was his name on the death certificate.

We go up to the third floor. I explain to another receptionist that I'm here to see Dr Gomez. She asks if I have an appointment. I don't. She doesn't know what to make of that, so she asks when I would like to make an appointment. Just as I'm about to respond, a grey-haired doctor opens the double doors opposite. He's studying a clipboard. He's grown a beard but I recognise him immediately. It's Dr Gomez.

I approach him. "Dr Gomez, I don't know if you remember me. I'm John Adamson. Can we talk?"

He looks up from his clipboard and his eyes widen. "Mr Adamson." He looks startled.

"You remember my wife, Christina? You treated her. I need to talk to you about what happened."

Dr Gomez steps back. He looks scared of me.

"I'm sorry, Mr Adamson, but I cannot talk now, and not here. I have a full schedule."

"When are you finished?"

"Err… five or six p.m. but…"

"Okay, it's fine. I will wait."

He says nothing more but glances at the receptionist, turns around and goes back through the doors to the emergency room.

I was hardly expecting a warm welcome but that was strange. Steve and I sit down and wait. The receptionist is on the phone, talking in a low voice and avoiding eye contact.

We're discussing our next move when three burly uniformed men approach us. They're not police – I'm guessing security. They ask us to accompany them. I ask why and one of them steps forward, takes my arm and says we are not permitted here without an appointment unless visiting a relative. I try to shake him off but he tightens his grip. Another guard takes Steve.

We're frogmarched downstairs and out of the main exit. One of them tells us to leave or they will call the police. The guards stand at the entrance with arms folded, glaring at us.

We go into the car park. Steve decides to call Richie, who says he'll come back to pick us up. Steve hangs up and tells me, "Richie said under no circumstances go back into the hospital. He said we don't want to end up in jail in this country."

Richie is right but if there was ever any doubt in mind about the diagnosis, there isn't anymore. There's no way we would be treated like that if we weren't on the right track. Dr Gomez looked really rattled.

When Richie arrives, I make sure the security guards see us getting into his car and driving away. I tell Richie to drive round the block and park outside the hospital grounds.

"What's your plan, John?"

"I reckon we wait until Dr Gomez comes out and follow him. Hopefully then I can talk to him."

I'm sure tailing a doctor isn't Richie's preferred plan but he reluctantly agrees. We wait and watch the entrance. Someone of Gomez's stature probably drove to work and wouldn't use public transport. He may even have a chauffeur pick him up, as many of the rich do that for extra security in Quito.

After about an hour, Dr Gomez comes out of the hospital. He stands at the entrance, looking around. He looks nervous. He walks to the right and gets into a silver SUV. Richie is pleased he doesn't have a chauffeur as he says they're usually trained to watch for anything suspicious because of carjackings.

Richie drives like a local taxi driver – rarely keeping to one lane and weaving in between traffic. He hangs back from Gomez's car, which is driving steadily but not too fast. I get the feeling Richie has done this before.

We follow Gomez for a couple of miles. He's heading north to the edge of the city and takes a right up a hill. Richie nods. "I know where he's heading. Bellavista on the hill. A lot of the rich live up there."

Richie follows, keeping his distance because it's a quiet road. The area is familiar to me. I was here years ago when I first visited Quito, before meeting Christina. There's a pine forest and gallery of Guayasamín's art depicting the oppression of indigenous peoples. It's a beautiful place, but I have no time for sightseeing.

As we come over the brow of a hill, Gomez's SUV has already pulled up at a barrier, then drives through. Richie curses. "This is as far as we go, guys. That's a gated neighbourhood. We can't get in unless a resident clears it with security."

Richie parks opposite and we discuss what to do next. "Okay, John, let's think about this. You think

Gomez gave a false diagnosis, and his behaviour today backs that up. Do you think that's all he did?"

"What do you mean 'that's all'? That's bad enough."

"No, I mean do you think he was involved any further? Isn't it more likely he was pressured or threatened into that diagnosis by someone?"

"Yes, likely."

"Okay. So he's scared of being exposed and losing his job, but probably even more scared of telling the truth and putting himself in danger."

Richie suggests I leave Dr Gomez a message, telling him I know the diagnosis was inaccurate but making clear I want to find out who killed my wife, not blame him or the hospital.

I write something out in a notebook, telling him our conversation will be confidential and anonymous. Richie translates it and leaves his phone number. He puts it in an envelope, gets out the car and talks to the security guards, handing them a tip to deliver it to Gomez.

Now we wait.

Chapter 27

I'm having breakfast with Richie in the dining room of my hotel. Steve went out early to meet some contacts from an ecological foundation. I'd almost forgotten he had other work to do, but he wouldn't be much use hanging around with me waiting for a phone call.

Richie is telling me what it's like living here. "I love this place, man. The scenery is just spectacular, the people are great and there's every season in this country. If I get sick of the mountains, I can be on a beach in a few hours. And the women – I'm not surprised you got married. They're so gorgeous! Fiery though. My girlfriend can be jealous as hell. I have a nice life here but she wants to go to the States. She has this starry-eyed view, like it's all Tinseltown and drive-in movies, right?"

"That must be a pretty common view of the US here. Ecuador has a lot going for it, but could you imagine staying here and having a family?"

"That's it, man. I don't know. Sometimes it feels more dangerous in this city, but the crime rate is actually not much worse than the States. I don't worry about it too much now, but if I had kids, that would be different. I'd want to move somewhere quieter, but the work is in the cities."

Sometimes on dark winter days in London, Christina and I would talk wistfully about moving to Ecuador to escape the rat race and the British weather, but it was never a serious idea.

Richie's phone rings. He looks at the number and raises his eyebrows at me. "Could be him. I don't recognise the number."

He answers and nods, passing me the phone.

"Mr Adamson? Dr Gomez. I don't like being followed, but with respect for your loss, I give you five minutes."

"Okay, doctor. I just want to know the truth."

"The truth? The truth is I did everything I could to save your wife. I regret I could not."

"Thank you, I appreciate that. But I need to know why you diagnosed dengue if it was not the cause of death."

"That was the official diagnosis."

"And unofficially?"

"The evidence was... unclear."

"Then why was it on the death certificate?"

There's silence for a moment. "A decision by the hospital."

"Why?"

"I don't know and I cannot say. You do not use my

name at all, is that clear?"

"Yes, okay."

"I think there was pressure."

"Pressure from who?"

"Governments possibly, but I don't know. I was given clear instructions."

"And you followed them?"

"Mr Adamson, with respect, you do not know this country. Some things I cannot question, even if I don't like them."

"If it wasn't dengue, then what do you think killed Christina?"

"I cannot be sure. Her symptoms were consistent with a high level of toxicity, but I did not test for it."

"What about the autopsy?"

"That was someone from outside, I believe. Mr Adamson, I cannot tell you more and I hope you keep your promise not to involve me. I will maintain the official diagnosis if asked."

"I won't use your name. I just want to find out who did this."

"I'll give you some advice. The answer is not at the hospital; it is in the *Oriente*. That is where your wife became ill. But Mr Adamson, you should take care. I wish you luck and again, sorry for your loss. Please do not contact me again."

He hangs up. I relay the conversation to Richie.

"I'm sorry, John, but looks like you were right. The diagnosis was a lie."

I take little satisfaction in being right but at least I no longer doubt my convictions. 'Toxicity', the doctor said. Poison. The thought horrifies me. The pain she must have gone through, and the whole time I was on the other side of the world.

I need some time alone to process this. I tell Richie I'll call him later and I go back to my room, thinking over what Dr Gomez said. Pressure from governments? Richie mentioned the owner of the hospital had connections with the government here, but Gomez said 'governments' – plural. I wonder if he meant the British government too. That might explain why Campbell was there, which is something I still can't figure out, although he doesn't even officially work for the British government.

The doctor said the answers are in the jungle. That's where Christina was poisoned and that's where I need to go next. I know it could be dangerous, but I'm like a moth to a flame.

Chapter 28

First impressions of Lago Agrio are that it deserves its bad reputation. Steve and I caught an hour-long flight from Quito. The flight was half full, mainly with locals and a few backpackers, no doubt on a jungle excursion.

Stepping off the plane, it's a different world from the mountains. It's mid-morning but already very hot, and a heavy humidity hangs in the air. We take a Jeep taxi into the town and a deluge comes from nowhere. Rain so hard I can hardly see the potholed road in front of us. I feel the regular bumps though.

The taxi drops us outside Café Mario, where our guide Ernesto has arranged to meet us. A voluptuous woman in tight denim shorts approaches me as I get out of the cab. "*Papito*, you want fun?" She's plastered in far too much make-up.

She looks from me to Steve and smiles. "You too?"

Steve raises his eyebrows. "Not here for fun, *Señorita*."

She pouts, then hisses through her teeth and crosses the street.

In the café, I can feel all eyes on us as we sit down at a table. Two *gringos* in this town stick out from a mile away. We're a long way from Quito.

Richie couldn't come. He said he had other work, but he also warned us about the last time he came here to investigate problems along the border with Colombia, ten miles to the north. He had to leave abruptly after being threatened, he thinks by a cartel. He told us, "Stay in the café, don't wander around town. Best if you're in and out of Lago Agrio quickly. Don't stay long and definitely don't stay overnight."

I haven't had much appetite for the few days we've been in Ecuador but Steve certainly has. He's licking his lips as he looks over the menu. "I fancy a big breakfast. Who knows what we'll have to eat in the jungle. Look, they have *guanta*. Richie said that's a big rat. Maybe later?" He makes a mock retching sound and laughs.

I'm glad Steve is here. He knows how serious this is, but his humour helps break the tension sometimes. We order coffee and *humitas* – a plate of steamed mashed corn with cheese that was Christina's favourite. She used to make them occasionally. It was time-consuming but worth the wait. They're delicious.

An indigenous man in a baseball cap walks in and spots us. "Mr Adamson? Mr Hartley?" Ernesto introduces himself, sits down and orders a coffee. He's dressed in jeans and a t-shirt. I hadn't exactly expected him to be bare-chested and carrying a blowgun, but it reminds me that Western culture reaches the farthest corners of the world.

He leans forward and speaks in a low voice. "I think Richie told you we don't stay long. Not too safe. Only *petroleros, narcos* and *putas* here, so finish your breakfast and then we leave."

He takes out a map. "We drive east for about an hour to Río Aguarico, then a few hours by boat east on the river. There is not much left of the Jaguarcocha community now, but we can talk to those that are still there. Most important, you need to stay with me and look like tourists, not reporters. That would attract too much attention from the wrong people. Take pictures, look excited, you know."

On cue, Steve takes out a Panama hat he bought in Quito and grins.

"Perfect," says Ernesto. "You look like a typical *gringo* tourist."

It's a relief to leave Lago Agrio and get my first glimpse of primary rainforest. I've never ventured this deep into the jungle before, only to the edges of the region near Puyo, further south.

Ernesto explains that some locals have started taking eco-tourists on 'toxic tours' to see the pollution, something Steve is keen to report on. The amount of oil spilt in this area is staggering, according to Ernesto – equivalent to thirty times the ten million gallons spilled in the Exxon Valdez disaster in the late 1980s. The pipeline runs parallel to the side of the road, and Ernesto stops for a few minutes to point out pools of black.

192

"They don't even record most spills anymore. It's constant. This oil you see could have been here for months or could have been spilt yesterday. The ground beneath the pipeline has been black for as long as I can remember."

Half an hour further on, Ernesto stops and leads us a few metres from the road to a series of tributaries running into a lagoon. He tells Steve to place his hand in the water. When Steve takes it out, his hand is completely black, covered in sticky tar. I take a photo. Ernesto hands him a cloth and Steve scrubs at his hand, but it's not easy to clean.

Ernesto tells us to listen. "You hear? It's too quiet. No birds. When I was a child, this lake was heaven for birdwatching. There are no birds now. They either died or flew deeper into the jungle."

I'm now seeing this place through Christina's eyes. I'm reminded of her post about the journey to the kapok tree and the lifeless silence she found there.

Steve fires a lot of questions at Ernesto during the rest of the drive, scribbling notes. He's in full reporter mode. We reach the small ramshackle town of Tarapoa. Ernesto parks and leads us down to a jetty into a motorised canoe. If I were a tourist, this is where I'd get excited, journeying into the heart of darkness on a river filled with alligators and anacondas. Steve doesn't need to act the part of an enthusiastic tourist – he's delighted to see the Amazon jungle for the first time, snapping away with his camera, pointing out monkeys in the

193

trees.

As we speed up, a fresh breeze dries the sweat from my forehead and I close my eyes. I open them again as the sun burns through the clouds and lights up the forest. I've never seen so many shades of green. The colours change every time our canoe rounds a corner. Ernesto points out a huge kapok tree towering over the canopy that lines the river bank. It dominates the landscape. No wonder it's considered sacred.

For a moment I imagine this is a place where time has stood still, but then a motorboat rounds a corner and heads straight towards us. It veers off to the left, passing within a few metres. The men in the boat wearing orange jackets don't even acknowledge us but stare impassively. Our canoe rocks hard from the waves their boat creates.

Ernesto curses and slows down. "Oil workers. They never smile at us because we get in their way. They have no soul. They sold it long ago."

I lose track of how long we're on the river, but it's several hours later when Ernesto docks on a small beach and we disembark. We walk up a mud path through some trees to a clearing. There are about a dozen wooden stilt houses with thatched roofs. Ernesto explains that the stilts are to keep the houses habitable during heavy rains and floods. Behind the houses is a circular lake.

Two women come out from a house and greet Ernesto in Kichwa. "*Kawsankichu.*" Ernesto talks with them. They seem to know each other. Then he gestures to me.

The women approach me and one of them clasps my hands in hers. There are tears in her eyes. She says, "Christina *sumak*, Christina *sumak*." Ernesto tells me this means 'beautiful'. I ask Ernesto for the word for thank you and say, "*Pakrachu*."

Her name is Samai. She won't let go of my hands and it begins to feel awkward. I don't feel I can share my grief with a stranger, but this woman must have spent a lot of time with Christina in her last few months, so we have an unspoken connection.

She indicates for us to sit on a bench on the balcony of the house and serves us green tea. Ernesto tells me it's *guayusa*, drunk to increase energy and improve concentration. It's often served in the morning for the people to interpret their dreams of the previous night. They take dreams very seriously and apparently use them to make plans and decisions.

I can't say I'm keen to reflect on my own dreams. I only have two at present: Christina is dying and I'm powerless, or Christina is alive and none of this happened, which is briefly blissful until I wake up. I don't know which dream is worse.

As we sit drinking, Steve asks Ernesto why the village is called Jaguarcocha. He's hoping to see a jaguar, although he knows they are incredibly rare.

Ernesto replies, "It's interesting you ask because some of the tribes believe the tea you're drinking contains the spirit of the jaguar and that's why it gives people the sight. Amazon people worship the jaguar as a god. It's the greatest of all hunters for it can hunt on land, in trees and in water. The word 'jaguar' means 'he who kills with one blow'. Only the anaconda can challenge the jaguar, but its main threat comes from humans, of course."

He continues. "According to the villagers, many centuries ago, the tribe wanted to settle here beside the lake but some of them were terrified because they had seen a jaguar drinking on the far side. The tribe had a meeting and agreed that the far side of the lake was the jaguar's territory and they would not venture there. They would also never leave the village at night, when the jaguar hunted. Every month they would capture a tapir alive and leave it wounded on the border of the jaguar's territory as an offering. And so an understanding grew between the tribe and the jungle god. The villagers lived for many centuries in harmony with the jaguar and no villagers were ever harmed. This harmony only ended with the arrival of oil and mining. No villager has seen a jaguar for many years. They believe it must have fled deeper into the forest."

It's a sad end to an initially comforting story. Steve looks disappointed that he's unlikely to see a jaguar, although given it's the largest cat in the Americas, I remind him that seeing one up close might be the last thing he ever does.

Ernesto tells me that Nina, a widow of one of the

tribal leaders, is coming to talk with me tomorrow morning. She's been spending more time deeper in the jungle because of receiving threats. He thinks she will know more about what happened at the village meeting months ago.

As I look out over the lake, I notice a young girl sitting on the banks scrubbing clothes. She can't be more than twelve. There's something familiar about her. I watch her for a while before I realise what it is – the light blue blouse she's wearing is Christina's. It was one of her favourites. She must have given it to the girl, unless Christina left some of her clothes in the village when she was taken to the hospital. I had wondered if Christina left anything here and was hoping to find not only keepsakes but also her notebook and camera, which could contain vital clues.

When the girl walks back up to the village, I ask Ernesto to ask Samai about the blouse. She nods and explains that Christina gave some of her clothes to the local girls. I reassure her that they should keep them.

She also says Christina left her backpack here but men came to the village and took it away. The men claimed it was to send it back to her family. I ask if she knew who the men were but she says no. The villagers were frightened of them because they came with guns. This is a real blow. They must have taken any evidence in Christina's notebook and on her camera roll.

Samai tells me nobody has stayed in Christina's room out of respect, so I ask her to take me there. The cabin is a few hundred metres away, overlooking the lake. Samai opens the door. It's a simple, musty room with a bed, mosquito net, small wooden table and bench. Samai stoops and opens a drawer under the table and shows me. There are some of Christina's clothes, so the men hadn't taken everything. Samai places a hand on my shoulder and leaves.

The clothes are mainly blouses, t-shirts and shorts. I find a long blue skirt that Christina wore often. I carefully refold it and put it in my bag. The rest I will leave for the villagers.

As I look outside the cabin, it's getting late and the sun is going down. I know Christina would never have missed a sunset. I remember the first time we watched it together in the mountains, just a few days after we first met. She lent her head on my shoulder and all felt right in my world for the first time in my life.

I sit at the cabin threshold and watch. I know instinctively this is where she used to sit to watch the colours stretch across the sky. The dusk chorus begins with sporadic birdsong combined with the hiss of cicadas. I sit and close my eyes to listen. When I open them again, the colours have changed, oranges giving way to deep reds and purples. It's a privilege to experience a sunset in the Amazon jungle.

As the light dims, I lie down on the bed and put my head on the pillow. Amid the mustiness, there's a faint scent of lavender. It must be the essential oil that Christina put on her pillow every night, just as she did in England. I sit up and press the pillow to my face. As I place it back on the bed, something is on my face. It's a single strand of hair, long and dark. It must be Christina's. I fetch a sheet of tissue and carefully wrap it up. And then the tears come.

Chapter 29

I hardly slept last night. I spent much of the night turning everything over in my mind. I've never slept in such complete darkness. There is no light here at night. I couldn't even see my feet as I stepped across the cabin floor to the bathroom, hoping to avoid all the arachnids my imagination could conjure.

The smell of cooking is wafting across to my cabin this morning so I make my way over to where I can see Steve and Ernesto. As I approach the house, I see a woman sitting with Samai. There are two young children at her feet and she's breastfeeding a third.

Samai introduces me and to my surprise, this is Nina. She's a lot younger than I expected, no older than mid-twenties. I still find it difficult to acknowledge beauty in anyone other than Christina without feeling pangs of guilt, but Nina is very beautiful. Long black hair with eyes to match. She smiles at me, but there's sadness in her expression.

"I'm very sorry for the loss, Mr Adamson."

I'm a bit taken aback that she addresses me in

English. "I'm also sorry for your loss."

"I speak some English. First, our people learnt Spanish, language of *conquistadors*. Now we learn English, language of their masters."

We agree to talk after breakfast. It occurs to me it's the first time since Christina's death that I've met someone who shares my grief at the loss of a spouse.

I sit down with Steve and Ernesto for a breakfast of fruit. Steve is tucking into some eggs and enthusing about his night walk to tarantula holes and conga ant nests. He got up before dawn to do some birdwatching too. I'm glad he's enjoying himself, as there's so much to experience here.

After breakfast, Ernesto and I join Nina, who is sitting by the lake. Ernesto tells me she prefers to speak Kichwa with him translating so she can be sure of using the right words. I ask her to tell me about the meeting and how Christina became unwell. She is quiet for a moment, gazing over the lake.

"My husband Yaku called a meeting with the leaders of three neighbouring villages. Everything was very bad with the miners invading and polluting more and more of our territory. Children were getting ill from bathing in polluted rivers. Some babies were even stillborn, but thankfully not mine.

"There was pressure on the whole community to move to government-built housing projects on polluted land where nothing would grow. We had lost income from tourists staying away, and some of the younger men were tempted to leave to work in oil or mining with promises of big money. Yaku knew it could not continue. Either we resisted or our community would die.

"He knew we could not fight the invaders with spears against guns, but he had hope after an American lawyer visited and wanted to help us fight in the courts. Yaku thought this could be our best path but he wanted the villages to work together, something which had been difficult before because of so much disagreement.

"Christina saw what the miners were doing and was very upset. She wanted to help. She was a good soul."

Nina looks up at the sky and makes a motion with her hands like a bird flying away, whispering something I cannot hear. Ernesto tells me it's a form of prayer.

"The meeting was meant only for the leaders but Christina asked Yaku if she could join them at the end and he agreed. Yaku told me the meeting went better than expected. Two of the other leaders were reluctant at first because they'd been threatened but it was decided by majority to work with the lawyer. Everyone seemed happy after the meeting.

"It was not until the middle of the night that Yaku fell ill. It came very suddenly. He was breathing heavily and he was burning hot to touch. We called the shaman to help but the curse was too strong. He died in my arms the next day."

Nina is silent for a while, bowing her head and stroking her baby's head. I ask Ernesto to ask what she means by the 'curse'.

She continues. "At first I had no idea what had happened, but now I think I know. My husband was a good man but he made enemies. In our village there was a young man called Marcelo. From a young age, he was not like the other boys. Many of the men, including my husband, did not treat him well. He spent less and less time in the village. I thought he would leave completely but he remained with us. He did go to Lago Agrio more often though. One day, he came back with money and an expensive cell phone. He wouldn't tell me where he got it. I believe he was in contact with the miners.

"The evening of the meeting, he seemed eager to help prepare the food and drink, so I let him. Later on, I thought I saw him put something in the *chicha*, but at the time I did not think anything more about it.

"When Marcelo saw Christina had joined the meeting and was drinking with the leaders, he became very upset. You see he liked Christina very much. She was very kind to him, as she was to everyone. I think she understood him and accepted him.

"When Christina fell sick, it was Marcelo who took her to town. He did not even ask us before taking her. I think he contacted the authorities and she was taken to hospital. He never returned to the village after that and I never saw him again."

"So you think he put something in the drink?"

"Yes, it is the only explanation. Everyone in the meeting drank the *chicha*. Everyone except my son. He is very small so he could not. All the adults died, but my son is alive. For that I am thankful."

"Do you have any idea where Marcelo went?"

"I heard he went to Quito to live the way he wanted. I also heard he uses his nickname 'Chelo' now."

Chelo. That name is familiar. Where did I see it? Then I remember – the username of the comments on Christina's last blog post was 'Chelomimi'. That warning and the final message: '*Paz en tu tumba*'. Nina said Marcelo had a cell phone. It must have been him.

So Christina was in the wrong place at the wrong time; she wasn't even supposed to die. It feels even worse to know this – it was so avoidable.

I've come all this way to the jungle to find answers and now I need to go back to Quito to find Christina's killer. Not only Marcelo though. I need to know who got him to poison the leaders.

I remember Christina's other post that she didn't publish. She mentioned a man named 'Tonio'. She said she'd learnt not to trust him and thought he was somehow involved in acquiring territory for mining.

I ask Nina, "Do you know a man named Tonio? Christina mentioned in her writing he might be involved."

For the first time, Nina looks afraid. "I do not know this man personally but I have heard of him. He is very rich and money buys power here. I hear that men in Lago Agrio do things for him. I think he is a *gringo*."

A foreigner? With a name like Tonio, I'd assumed he

was from Ecuador. Ernesto tells me he can make some enquiries about this man, but we will need to be careful. He says it would be better if he does this himself because a foreigner asking questions would draw too much attention.

I ask Nina what she plans to do. She says, "I am afraid for my children. I cannot leave them as orphans, but neither can I forgive myself if I don't stand up for our people and for Mother Earth. Our world used to be in perfect balance, but now the balance is gone and there is chaos. Nothing will be right until balance is restored."

I hope I haven't put Nina in even more danger. She came to the village today specifically to talk with me. We say our goodbyes and she takes her children to a boat heading downriver where she feels safer. It's unspeakable that a widowed mother of three is in fear of her life for trying to save her community.

I can't stay another night here. It's too difficult for me to be in the place where Christina was poisoned. I already suspected what happened, but I'm shell-shocked to discover she wasn't targeted at all. She accidentally drank poison meant for the leaders. It was so unnecessary. Her death was a horrible mistake. Part of me wants to find this Marcelo and rip him apart.

I ask Ernesto to take us back to Lago Agrio. He says it's best to head straight to the airport and bypass the town completely. Steve contains his disappointment at spending so little time in the jungle, but he's already filled an entire notebook and taken hundreds of photos.

Steve and Ernesto talk more about environmental issues on the journey back, but I zone out of the conversation. I can't help noticing Ernesto keeps looking in the rear-view mirror though. He looks worried. I look behind us. There's a large black SUV with a blacked-out windscreen driving close to us.

Ernesto drives into the airport and parks directly outside the departure gate where there are security guards. We get out and walk straight into the airport. Steve is confused at the hurry. I don't say anything.

We book an afternoon flight to Quito and head to the gate. I look behind me and see two men standing at the entrance watching us. They linger for a few minutes. I think they want to make sure we've clocked them before they leave. It will certainly be a relief to get out of Lago Agrio.

As we sit on the runway, I'm thinking about my next move when Steve nudges me. "Look over there! That looks just like the mural. You remember the photograph at the first killing?"

I look over to where he's pointing – a wall on the perimeter of the airport. It's hard to see clearly at this distance. Steve retrieves binoculars from his bag and looks, then hands them to me. I focus in and Steve is right. It's either the same mural or an exact copy.

"Didn't you say the mural was in Colombia though?"

"Yes, but this looks the same. There must be more of them. I wonder how long it's been here. I'll ask Ernesto to look into it." Steve zooms in with his camera.

I stare at the mural through the binoculars as the plane's engines start. The bones and ashes on the left; the forest, children and wildlife on the right; and the writing in the soil: '*De sus cenizas, crecerán brotes verdes*'.

Whoever painted this must believe that even amid so much death, there is still hope.

Chapter 30: El Ruido

They called him '*El Rudo*' – 'the rude one'. The nickname reflected his abrupt, unfriendly manner and was similar to his real name, which locals found hard to pronounce. He was never much of a talker. They paid him for his military skills, not his conversation skills, and they paid top dollar.

He'd long ago left the US military for a lucrative career as a mercenary. His latest mission was in the Colombian jungle, working with paramilitaries to target drug traffickers and FARC rebels. He impressed his unit with his sniper abilities and prowess at sneaking up on enemies.

His nickname soon changed to '*El Ruido*' – 'the noise', in ironic deference to his unnervingly silent movement. His comrades used to say that if enemies heard *El Ruido*, it would be the last thing they ever heard. His prey usually suspected nothing until a bullet hit their chest or a knife slashed their throat.

El Ruido had many tactics. Sometimes he was an alligator under the surface of the river, gliding through the water unseen. On other missions, he was a jaguar, hiding in the foliage waiting for nightfall. His preferred position though was up in the trees with leaves and branches obscuring him, from where he could pick off targets with ease.

Factors he couldn't control though were luck and betrayal. On his last mission, everything initially appeared to be going to plan. He and his unit had identified a rebel camp and planned an ambush. He took a position high in a tree, but when gunfire erupted below, it was clear that instead of leading an attack, his comrades were themselves being ambushed. The rebels must have known they were coming. Someone had tipped them off.

He watched the carnage below. Half his unit were already dead before he'd even fired a shot. The rebels were advancing within range, so he picked off several with precision, but they soon realised someone was shooting at them from the trees and fired dozens of rounds upwards. *El Ruido* winced as a bullet hit his arm and another his leg. He held on tightly to the branch, focusing on staying conscious as he knew the fall could kill him.

When the shooting stopped, he heard the rebels move off in the direction of the river where his unit had disembarked. No doubt they would seize the boats and block his escape route.

He cut off strips of his jacket and tied them tightly around the wounds to slow the bleeding. He was lucky these were flesh wounds and the bullets had passed through, but he knew infection was his biggest threat. He was far from a hospital and needed medical attention quickly. A few days in the jungle and he could die from infected wounds, but getting back to the nearest town meant slipping past the rebels. That was nearly impossible, especially with his injuries hampering his movement.

Trying to block out the pain, he waited for hours in the tree, hoping to hear the rebels leave, but they did not. He couldn't stay there much longer in case he passed out, so he started to make his way down. It was torturously slow and painful. He flicked the safety on his rifle and threw it down to the ground. He tried to climb down the trunk of the tree, his arm and leg in agony, but lost his grip and fell twenty feet, hitting the ground so hard he lost consciousness.

When he woke up, it was dark. There was still no sign of the rebels. His wounds wreaked havoc on his senses and he could only guess at the direction of the Brazilian border. That was his best chance. He knew it would be a few miles to the east and crossing was largely uncontrolled. If he could make it across, he'd be safe from the rebels at least, although he had no idea how far it was to the nearest settlement.

He took advantage of the darkness to cover as much ground as his wounds would allow. He'd have to be wary of jaguars because this was their hunting time. He walked for hours until sunrise confirmed he was going in the right direction. His instincts had not deserted him, but he couldn't be sure if he'd already crossed the border. He was becoming feverish and his water bottle was nearly empty. He needed to rest, so he found a sheltered hollow and covered himself in foliage.

He didn't know if he was dreaming or hallucinating. There were voices talking in a language he didn't understand. He tried in vain to resist as he felt them prise away his rifle, before he was carried away. The pain from his injured limbs kept him drifting in and out of consciousness.

In his dreams, he saw a beautiful woman with long black hair, almond eyes and coffee-coloured skin. When he woke up, she was looking at him. He wondered if she was an angel and he was already dead. It would surprise him to be among angels after all the people he'd killed.

He became more aware of his surroundings – the wooden cabin and the straw mattress he lay on. As he tried to sit up and lift his leg, he felt a spasm of pain. The woman placed her hand on his shoulder and shook her head, and he understood he should not move. His wounds were covered in a sticky paste. He couldn't resist the urge to look, but again the woman shook her head.

They couldn't speak each other's language so they used sign and gesture instead. Her name was Pacha. From his scant knowledge of Kichwa, he knew this meant 'Earth'. He pointed at the ground as he said her name and she smiled in recognition. He tried to ask her if they were in Brazil or Colombia, but she did not understand.

Pacha tended him for days, mopping his brow and keeping him hydrated and fed on a simple diet of rice and fruit. Soon his fever and delirium began to subside. She cleaned his wounds daily, singing as she did so. That was what he looked forward to the most. Her voice soothed his pain as much as the paste. He didn't know what the paste consisted of, but he could see no signs of infection or gangrene, so it was indeed keeping the wound clean. He was lucky.

He was soon well enough to get up and sit at the threshold of the cabin to see the community that had saved him. The men, women and children were bare-chested with red cloths tied around their waists, their torsos and faces painted with red dye.

Pacha had kept herself apart from the rest of the tribe for a quarantine period. This was the law if any outsider arrived because stories of white men bringing sickness were passed down the generations. After a full cycle of the moon though, he was invited to leave his cabin and sit with the tribe.

The leader of the village, Raoni, spoke some Portuguese and asked him how he came to be in his territory. He was relieved to discover that he had in fact crossed the border. His Portuguese was worse than his Spanish but he laboured to explain about fighting *narcos* and how he had crossed the border to escape them. Raoni seemed satisfied with this. He said the *narcos* were bad people.

Raoni recognised him as a fellow warrior and instructed the men to demonstrate how they hunted and defended themselves with blowguns and spears. He was astonished at their precision with such basic weapons. His attempts to hit a target with a spear were poor at first, but he proved quite adept with a blowgun. That made Pacha smile.

Pacha always served his food and sat opposite him at mealtimes. They communicated mainly with signs but he began to pick up some of the village language. He had never seen a woman so beautiful and so free. He did not dare to embrace her though, mindful of offending her family.

The longer he stayed, the less he desired to return to the life of killing for money that he'd known for so long. He felt a peace in this place he'd never experienced before.

Chapter 31

I don't know how I imagined my investigation progressing when we arrived in Ecuador, but bar-hopping in Quito was not how I saw it panning out. We're sitting outside on Plaza Foch, the main square and centre of nightlife in the New Town. It's past ten p.m. and getting busy.

Steve is tucking into some shrimp ceviche while Richie is sipping his beer and appreciating the young women walking past. You wouldn't know he has a girlfriend, the way he's looking them up and down. I can't blame him though; there are beautiful people wherever I look. I should know – I fell in love with one.

Richie knows a lot of people in this city and has asked a few gay friends for the most popular places. He tells me the scene has grown in recent years and Mariscal district draws gay people from around the country, often fleeing prejudice and violence. From what Nina told me, this must be what drew Marcelo here.

I don't have much to go on, but I've trawled through

Christina's blog again. There's a sullen-looking young man with long dark hair sat next to her in one of the photos. He fits the description Nina gave me.

This is the second night in a row we've tried to find Marcelo. Not much luck last night, although one of the doormen outside gay bar Eldorado told Richie that 'Chelo' sounded familiar and we should come back tonight when it's busier.

The line for the club is already long at eleven p.m. Inside, there's loud techno and a mixed crowd of mainly young local gay men with a few older foreigners standing at the bar. Steve, the blond Adonis, is getting a lot of attention and it's amusing on an otherwise tense evening to see him regularly rebuff propositions, holding up his wedding ring to confused reactions.

As the place fills up, the DJ cuts the music and announces the start of a cabaret to loud cheers. We watch a succession of acts, some doing dance routines, others belting out songs. I don't see Marcelo though. I walk around the club during the performances, scouring for someone who fits the description.

There's a small group sat right at the back, sipping cocktails. A young man with long dark hair is among them. I approach the table and he breaks off from his conversation. He looks at me and his smile disappears. It's Marcelo, and he seems to recognise me.

He gets up and runs. I try to grab him but his companions bar my way. He disappears through a door in the back.

I hadn't considered that Marcelo might recognise me, but of course Christina had photos. If she got on well with him, she may have shown him what I look like.

I rush back to get Richie and Steve and we head through the same door. It leads to a fire escape. I catch a glimpse of Marcelo running down an alley. We take off after him. He's moving quite fast but Richie is faster and after a couple of blocks, he wrestles him to the ground.

Marcelo shouts, "*No me maten, no me maten* – don't kill me!"

As he lies on the floor shaking, I look down at the man who poisoned my wife and for the first time in my life, I want to do serious harm. Before I know what I'm doing, I lunge towards him, but Steve pulls me back.

"John, no. Calm down!"

I'm breathing hard. I really want to hurt him.

Steve grabs me by both shoulders and looks me in the eyes. "John, this is not you. It won't bring Christina back."

Richie pulls Marcelo up and tells him in Spanish we just want to talk and find out what happened to Christina, then we won't hurt him.

"Right, John?" Richie looks at me intently. I see the terror on Marcelo's face, take a deep breath and nod. I know Steve's right.

"Okay, we talk. But you tell me everything, understand?"

Richie leads Marcelo away from the busy area to

where his car is parked. Marcelo hesitates before getting in the back seat with Richie still holding his arm. I get in the front with Steve.

Marcelo doesn't speak much English so Richie translates. "I assume you know who I am. My wife Christina died along with four of your community's leaders in Jaguarcocha."

Marcelo sobs with his head in his hands.

"The villagers told us it was you. We know you gave them poison."

Marcelo flinches at the word '*veneno*'. It takes him a long time to speak.

"I adored Christina. It was a mistake."

"What do you mean – a mistake?"

He doesn't answer.

"You were seen putting something in the drink. What was it?"

He looks at me briefly, then looks away. "They told me it would only make them sick."

"Who? Who gave you the poison?"

Marcelo seems to be thinking about what to say. I'm starting to get angry again. I don't want to give him time to think up any lies.

"We said we won't hurt you if you tell us everything. If you don't…"

Finally, Marcelo says, "It was a man in Lago Agrio. If I tell you, you must never say you know this from me. They will kill me."

"Agreed. What man?"

"I don't know his name, but he lied to me."

"Tell me about this man. What happened in Lago Agrio?"

"I met him there when I was fetching supplies. He bought me lunch and gave me a new phone. He said he wanted information."

"Information on what?"

"He wanted to know what the villagers were going to do – if they would accept the offer to move or if they would resist. When I sent him messages about the meeting, he told me to come to town again to talk."

"So you went? What happened?"

"This time he took me upstairs to a room, he said for privacy, but then he pulled out a knife. He said he would kill me if I didn't do what he said. He gave me a small bottle and told me to put it in the drinks of the leaders. He said *chicha* tastes so bad, they wouldn't notice.

"I told him I didn't want to kill anyone, but he told me it would only make them sick for a few days. Then they would believe it was a curse and do as the company said. He lied! I swear I didn't know it would kill them. I never wanted to hurt Christina, you must believe me."

Marcelo looks at me, pleading. I ignore this and continue my questions.

"Which company? Did you get this man's name?"

"I don't know. He never gave me any names."

"What did he look like?"

"He was a white Ecuadorian, I think maybe from Quito. But I saw him talking to another man, a *gringo*, when I was leaving."

"A foreigner?"

"Yes. He was tall, white, rich-looking. I could tell by the way the man had his eyes down that the *gringo* was in charge."

This might be the 'Tonio' Christina mentioned. The man Nina was afraid of.

"Do you know a man named Tonio?"

Marcelo frowns. "No, but I've heard the name. Maybe it was him. I don't know."

I need to find out who this man is. Maybe I can get to him through the first man Marcelo met.

"Do you still have the first man's phone number?"

"After what happened, he called and told me to delete all our messages and not to talk to anyone or he would find me."

Richie tells Marcelo to give him his phone, which he does reluctantly. Richie spends a few minutes scrolling through the call history and tells Marcelo to point out the number. He notes it down, takes Marcelo's number and gives the phone back.

Marcelo looks more worried now. "But you must not contact him! He will know I talked to you. Please, I'm so sorry. I will never forgive myself."

He puts his head in his hands again. "I will never stop hurting for Christina. The others though, they never treated me like one of their people. They used to hold me down and put fire ants on me. The bites were agony for days. They believed it would stop me being who I

219

am. The leaders did nothing to stop them."

He was badly treated no doubt, but I don't want to hear any more excuses from Marcelo. I don't want to spend another moment with him, otherwise I might lose control again. We've got everything we're going to get, so I tell Richie to tell him we're done. Marcelo looks relieved and gets out of the car.

Richie says we should follow up on the leads tomorrow. "I don't know about you guys, but I need a drink. Wanna go to Bungalow 6? It's a good place."

Richie is a great help, but tact isn't his strong point. I've just interrogated the man who poisoned my wife after nearly assaulting him. The last thing I want is a beer, so I tell them to go ahead without me.

We're only a couple of blocks from the hotel, so I walk back. The streets are very quiet away from the main plaza. I'm suddenly aware of being alone on a dark street after midnight. I can hear footsteps behind me. I turn around but don't see anyone. I'm sure there's somebody there though. I quicken my pace and I'm relieved to turn a corner to my hotel. I turn the key, go inside and breathe again.

Chapter 32

I get up early after another sleepless night. So many thoughts were spinning round my head as I replayed the encounter with Marcelo. I wonder what would have happened if Steve hadn't held me back and how far I would have gone. It's hard to say. I was barely in control, that's for sure.

I know deep down that with the ineffective Ecuadorian justice system, and such scant evidence, it's hard to see how I can get justice for Christina. I came here for some measure of closure but I fear I'm not going to get it.

I heard Steve fumbling around getting into his room next door around three a.m., so I'm sure he had a better night than me. I wouldn't have been good company and I don't begrudge him having fun. He's never been to South America before so it must be an adventure to sample the nightlife, as long as Richie didn't lead him too far astray.

When I go down to breakfast, the receptionist tells me there's a message for me. It's a folded handwritten note. It reads: 'Urgent, please come. Marcelo'. Underneath is an address. I ask the receptionist, who confirms it's in Quito, a few miles away. I ask if she remembers who left the message, but it was before her shift started. She asks if I want her to order a taxi, but I need to speak to Steve first.

I'm far from keen to see Marcelo again. It was hard enough to control myself last night, but maybe he's remembered something important.

I leave Steve to sleep for an hour before knocking on his door. I hear groaning and stumbling around. He answers, looking worse for wear.

"Had a good night, then?"

"Morning, mate."

"Not feeling so great?"

"No, it was mistake trying to keep up with Richie. He drinks like a fish."

"I've got some painkillers. I know you'd rather sleep it off but something came up."

I hand him the note. He squints at it. "Urgent? He wasn't exactly keen on talking last night."

"I need to go. He might have more information."

Steve doesn't argue. He can't face breakfast, so he gets dressed and we head out, taking a taxi north to the address near Parque Carolina. It's an old apartment block with an outside staircase.

I knock on apartment 4D and wait. There's no response. I'm already starting to get annoyed. I'd hoped never to see Marcelo again and now I'm calling at his apartment. I knock again harder and the door opens an inch. It's unlocked.

We go inside. There's a small kitchen with a table and chairs, and a door through to the back. It's a bedroom. The blinds are shut and it's dark but I can make out a shape in the bed.

"Marcelo?"

Nothing. I find a light switch – a decision I instantly regret.

Lying on the bed in front of us is Marcelo, his mouth hanging open, covered in blood. He's dead. Steve starts to heave and runs back out the door. I can hear him vomiting. It's a grim sight at any time but worse in Steve's state.

I force myself to look closer at Marcelo. It's hard to say exactly how he was killed. I thought initially his throat had been cut but there's no wound. He's holding an empty packet of pills. I can't read what they are. Maybe it was an overdose then.

As I move closer, my attention shifts to the bedside table. There's a piece of paper that reads: 'Green go – *gringo* go home'. Below the note on the table is a red blob of flesh. I look closer and now I feel like retching. Someone cut his tongue out.

Someone must have known he talked. We must have been followed. So I wasn't imagining it last night.

I get into reporter mode, take photos and pick up the note. It reminds me of the Liu killing – a crime scene for me to find, the victim's horrific expression and a cryptic

223

note.

I take one last look at the man who killed my wife before leaving the room. I don't feel in the least bit sorry for him. Something has changed in me, and I'm not sure I like it.

Steve is still coughing and spitting outside.

"You okay? I would have left you in bed if I'd known what we'd find."

I show him the note.

"Shit, John. That's a pretty clear threat."

"I know. I'm calling Richie."

I wake Richie up by the sounds of it. I fill him in on what happened.

"Jesus, man. Are you guys okay? You sure there's nobody else there?"

"We're fine. Well, Steve threw up last night's liquid dinner but aside from that…"

"He threw up? Not good, John. That's DNA at the scene. And Marcelo was chased by us very publicly last night. Get the hell out of there now! I'll meet you at your hotel."

It hadn't occurred to me before but setting us up would be an easy way to get rid of us. They wouldn't need to hurt us if we were languishing in a Quito jail.

We hurry down the stairs onto the street. As we turn the corner, a police car passes us going in the direction of Marcelo's apartment. That was a close call. We hail a cab and go back to the hotel.

Steve looks shaken. I forget sometimes that I'm used

to seeing bodies, but it's probably his first time seeing anything like that. I suggest a drink in the café.

Steve nurses his coffee. "John, you remember what I promised Alison? She said if there's any trouble I should come back, and I agreed. Well, finding the guy we talked to last night dead with his tongue ripped out and a threat to us to go home, I think that counts as very big trouble. I'm sorry, John, but I need to go back to England, and so should you."

I can't argue with him. I'm grateful he came because his company has made this trip less gruelling, but while I've already lost my family, his is back home. I don't want him taking more risks on my account.

"You're right, Steve. You should get a flight back as soon as you can. I'm not sure about me leaving though. I may stay a few more days. I've got leads from Marcelo on this man who threatened him and the other man Tonio. Maybe Richie can help. I can't just stop here."

Steve looks at me, shaking his head. "John, I have to be honest, I'm worried about you. You didn't seem affected at all by finding Marcelo brutally murdered. In fact, you looked almost… pleased. You had this odd smile on your face when you came out of there."

I wasn't aware of smiling. 'Pleased' isn't the right word, but maybe deep down I felt a type of justice was exacted. Part of me pitied Marcelo, but another part of me definitely wished him harm.

I don't know what to say to Steve, but I'm relieved when Richie walks in to break the awkward silence.

I show him the note. "Why does it say 'green go'?"

Richie considers it a moment. "The origin of the word *gringo* – the US army wore green. Mexicans used to say it to tell them to leave, then it kind of stuck."

Richie folds up the note and puts it away. "I'll get rid of it – it's blood-stained. We don't want any more evidence tying you to the scene."

He takes a deep breath. I know what's coming. "John, it's time you went home. I know this city and like I said before, the right guy from the black market will kill you for a few hundred bucks. You saw what happened to Marcelo – these guys mean business."

"But I'm not done, Richie. I need to find the men behind the poisoning."

"John, the man who poisoned your wife is dead. You can't set yourself against the entire mining industry here. It would likely end in a hail of bullets."

I don't want to stop now. I want all of them. It would be easier to do this with help, but it looks as though I'll have to do it alone.

Chapter 33

It's Easter week so getting a flight home has proven difficult for Steve. He's hoping to fly out the day after tomorrow. I still haven't decided if I'm going with him. If I do stay though, I won't get any more help from Richie. He said plainly he's not getting involved any further. He told me, "It's too dangerous and remember I live here, I can't just fly away."

We changed to a different hotel because the people following us clearly knew where we were staying. We've kept to our rooms, but today Steve needs to go to a travel agency to sort out his flight. He's annoyed they won't do it over the phone.

The agency is a few blocks from the hotel, near Plaza Foch. We head out in the afternoon. It's rainy and cold. It's odd how Quito with its bars, pubs and cold climate reminds me a little of London.

We're both tense. The street is eerily quiet. Once again, I get the feeling I'm being followed. I look around and see a man a hundred yards behind us. He turns and looks into a shop window. Am I being paranoid? I keep stealing looks behind, so I don't immediately notice a motorbike is coming towards us. It slows down as it approaches.

There are two men on the bike. They say something to each other and one of them points in our direction. I see the man on the back reach inside his jacket pocket. He's got a gun. I yell at Steve, "Get down!"

The shop window behind us smashes as a bullet rips through it. The man re-aims. Then I hear a bang from behind us. He flies backwards off the bike. The man I saw behind me is now running towards us. He's carrying a gun. Oh god, we're dead. I look back at the motorbike and the driver is helping his wounded partner up. He's been shot in the midriff. He shouts, "*Vamos*!" and they speed off.

I look across to Steve. He's on the floor in a pool of blood. It looks like a leg wound. I pray the bullet didn't hit an artery, otherwise he could be dead in minutes. The man rushes up to us, moves me out of the way and takes out a knife. I grab him by the arm instinctively but he shakes me off. "*Espera* – wait." He cuts Steve's jeans below the knee and ties a makeshift tourniquet around his thigh. He turns to me and gestures to the wound. "*Presión, presión*!" I press it. We need to get him to a hospital fast.

The man walks into the centre of the road and flags down a taxi. The driver looks across at us but then shakes his head. He's about to drive away when the man pulls out his gun and points it at the driver's head. He turns to the dashboard and reads aloud: "*José Miguel García Pinto, Cédula número 0860343266. Llevalos al hospital, ya!*"

He keeps his gun trained on the driver and beckons me. I help Steve into the back seat. The man steps back and glares at the driver. Something tells me he wouldn't think twice about pulling the trigger. The man looks me square in the face and says, "*Buena suerte*, John." He steps back and the driver presses the accelerator.

I can't worry right now about how the hell he knows my name. We need to get to the hospital. There's too much traffic though and the driver's going too slowly, so I shout at him to speed up. Steve has gone very pale. I keep talking to him, telling him he'll be fine and he'll get home to Alison and the kids soon.

We arrive at a hospital I don't recognise and I pull Steve out of the car. A male nurse helps me get him inside and puts him on a stretcher. I don't know the Spanish for bullet so I make a gun shape with my fingers.

They take him through to the emergency room, then the nurse comes back asking about insurance. Unbelievable. I hadn't even thought to get those details but both of us have an insurance card for the trip. I show mine and try to explain Steve has the same in his wallet.

The waiting is the worst part. I can't sit down. I pace around like a deranged bear in a zoo. I decide to call Richie and he says he'll come ASAP. All I can think is this is my fault. Steve came because of me. We should have left the moment I realised we were being followed. We could have just gone to the airport and taken any flight out of here, it wouldn't have mattered.

Richie walks in and I tell him what happened. He's quiet for a while, just shaking his head and swearing under his breath.

"That's a textbook hit in this city, using a moped for a quick getaway. Lucky that guy was there, otherwise you'd both probably be dead."

"It wasn't luck, Richie. I'm sure he was following us, and he knew my name too."

There was something familiar about this man. He spoke Spanish, but with an accent. I don't think it was his first language. I don't know who he was but all that matters now is Steve has to pull through.

We wait and wait. It's torturous. I won't be able to live with myself if he doesn't make it. Finally, the same nurse comes back through the doors and Richie talks with him. I see his shoulders relax and pray it must be good news. Richie tells me the bullet missed the artery by a whisker and passed straight through. They've stemmed the blood loss and are stitching him up. He's going to be okay. I can breathe again.

After giving me a moment to digest this, Richie puts his hands on my shoulders and says, "Look at me, John. As soon as Steve is discharged, you both get the next plane out of here. They won't think twice about organising another hit. You have to leave. No arguing."

I'm not arguing. I can't see any alternative. We go in

to see Steve a little later. He looks very pale and weak, but hasn't lost his sense of humour. "Better than the Sundance Kid, eh? Came to South America, got shot and lived to tell the tale!"

I force a smile. Richie wants to stay and get Steve out of the hospital tonight. He doesn't think it's safe. He has a friend who is a nurse and says we can stay at his place to make sure Steve is well enough before flying out.

After his bravado fades, Steve gets more emotional and tells me, "All I could think of was Alison and the boys, how I wanted to see them again. The thought of not seeing them again was too horrible to contemplate. I can't imagine how you feel, mate."

My nightmares have been reality for so long now, I can hardly remember how it felt when all was right in my world. My relief at Steve's recovery is mixed with a bucket load of guilt over the danger I put him in.

It's incredibly frustrating that I haven't identified who was really behind what happened to Christina, but I'm not giving up yet. I know Richie is right though. There's nothing for me here but death.

Chapter 34: El Ruido

As time passed, he settled into a routine in the village, accompanying the men each morning to go hunting, then spending afternoons and evenings with Pacha. He was proud to be included in hunts but mainly watched as the men expertly speared fish in the river and shot monkeys with blowguns. They hunted only as much as the village needed.

When he returned to the village though, he could feel something was wrong. Raoni was sitting in a semi-circle deep in conversation with other elders. In broken Portuguese, Raoni explained that men were trying to invade the village's territory. The situation had become more serious this time because one of the young warriors had apparently fired an arrow at the invaders in warning. Raoni was concerned they would come back with guns.

He did not sleep well that night, thinking of what to do, and the next day he went to Raoni and asked for his rifle. The villagers had not returned it to him since he was rescued. They were clearly afraid of guns. He told

Raoni he wanted to defend them in the event of an attack, but Raoni looked unhappy, so he didn't press the point.

Later that day, the men stationed as lookouts at the edge of the village returned with news that armed men were approaching. He went again to Raoni and repeated that he wanted to defend the village. Raoni reluctantly agreed and returned his rifle to him. After ascertaining which direction the invaders were coming from, he found a suitable tree a few hundred metres from the village and climbed to make his sniper's nest.

He heard shots in the distance. Soon afterwards, two of the men returned to the village carrying a third warrior who was clearly wounded. This stirred up fury among all the warriors and they armed themselves with spears, bows and arrows. He knew they would be no match for heavily armed men; it would be a massacre.

He heard shouts in Portuguese coming from the south – the invaders were not even bothering to approach quietly. Their arrogance would be their downfall.

He waited until he could see the group. There were at least eight, all armed with rifles. One of the men shouted to the warriors to lay down their weapons. When they refused, the men cocked their rifles. He did not wait for them to shoot first and he squeezed the trigger, hitting two men square in the chest before the others took cover. He managed to pick off a third before the men beat a hasty retreat.

When he was sure they had gone, he came down from

the tree to check on the villagers. Fortunately, nobody else had been shot, and the young wounded warrior was being tended to. It looked like he would recover.

Raoni thanked him for defending the village. Pacha rushed towards him and embraced him. Her father then stepped forward and pressed their hands together. He understood it meant their union had his blessing. They spent their first night together.

When he woke in the morning though, he was troubled. He knew these invaders would probably come back and in greater numbers. He may have made a bad situation worse.

Everything was calm for a while. He dared to hope the invaders had moved on to target a different territory and would leave the village alone. He resumed his routine of hunting during the day and spending evenings with Pacha. He started building a new cabin for them. Pacha's belly began to grow and he was delighted he was to become a father. He'd never imagined he would actually create life, having taken so many.

One day, he was hunting in a small group on the northern fringes of the village's territory. It had been a successful hunt but the men sensed something was wrong. They started to sniff the air. He could not smell anything but the men were sure it was smoke. The group decided to head back to the village immediately but the closer they got, the more visible the smoke became, until the air was thick with it.

As they emerged on a ridge overlooking the village a

few miles away, the devastation was clear to see. The whole forest was on fire with thick black smoke obscuring the sun. There was an ill wind fanning the flames.

He knew this could be no accident. The invaders were wreaking their vengeance. He felt a fear he had never known before. He was never scared for himself and had accepted he would probably not live a long life, but Pacha and his unborn child were down there somewhere. He could hear distant cries. He crashed forward in the direction of the village but within a few hundred metres, the heat became too intense. He couldn't breathe. The fire was between him and home. He coughed and heaved, covering his mouth and nose. It was of little use. The smoke was too thick.

He broke away from the other men and headed west to the river to try to reach the village that way. At least the water would protect him from the flames, but he'd have to take his chances with alligators. When he reached the river, it was filled with wildlife fleeing the flames. He saw several monkeys drowning. Heaven had turned to hell.

He waded along the river. The fire had not crossed to the forest on the opposite side, so he made his way along the far bank. As he got closer to the village though, the fire grew more intense. Flames leapt from tree to tree. He had never seen fire move so fast. The flames made it impossible for him to cross and find Pacha. He could do nothing but hope she had escaped. The smoke was so thick that he couldn't breathe. He tried to retreat but, starved of air, he lost consciousness.

When he woke up, the forest was silent. He was not burnt so he must have been saved by the river. He stumbled back to the water's edge, but on the other side, there was nothing but tree stumps and ashes.

There was still hope she might be alive. He couldn't see anyone at first, but when he waded across the river further down, he saw dozens of bodies floating. He thrashed through the water towards them. The first body he found was the village leader Raoni. He must have led his people to the river to try to escape.

He turned one body over and then another until he found her. Pacha was lying on her back in the water, her eyes closed. She didn't appear to be burnt but she wasn't breathing. He carried her to the riverbank and breathed in her mouth to try to give life to her and his child. He pushed her chest and kept breathing, but it was no good. She was gone.

He lay down on the mud and wept for the first time since he was a child, his head resting on Pacha's belly. Where once there was life, now there was none.

Slowly, he became aware of a sound – an animal panting. He looked across at the river and saw a jaguar barely ten metres from him. It crawled out of the water with great effort. He could see it was burnt, fur singed over half its body. It growled weakly before lying on the mud bank. The jaguar was so close to him, he could be dead in seconds, but the animal did not seem to even notice his presence. He wished it had the strength for one more kill, then he could join Pacha.

Inch by inch, he crawled towards the jaguar. Its eyes were glazing over. As he approached, the cat widened its eyes and looked at him. It tried to lift its head but its strength was gone.

He had never been this close to the god of the forest before. He placed his hand on the jaguar's huge body. It did not even flinch. Its life was ebbing away. He could feel its gigantic heart beat slower and slower until it beat no more.

As dawn broke, he dug a grave in the mud and returned Pacha to the earth. As he did so, he swore a terrible vengeance against the men who did this. He would not rest until he had killed them all, and killed their masters, one by one.

Chapter 35

It's been a few days since I got back. Three or four days – I'm not sure as I've spent most of it drunk. I was already heading for a tailspin, but the look Steve's wife Alison gave me at the airport was probably the last straw. It was unbearable. Steve was crying and hugging his boys while Alison just stared at me, shaking her head.

I've been so selfish. I'm a bad friend and a bad person. I couldn't look after my wife and now I nearly got my best mate killed. And what do I have to show for it? I don't feel better knowing what happened to Christina. I don't feel better knowing the man who poisoned her is dead either. I may never bring the people responsible to justice and none of this will bring her back anyway. She's still gone. For a short while, I had a purpose to keep my mind off reality. Now I feel like an empty shell again.

I went straight from the airport to the supermarket and bought as much booze as I could get my hands on – whisky, brandy, vodka, and I don't even like vodka. The cashier asked if I was having a party. As I collected the change, I told her, "No, but I might drink myself to oblivion!" She looked shocked. She'll get over it.

I don't remember much from the past few days, but I must have ended up in a bar on Saturday night. I woke up on the floor in some woman's flat. I couldn't remember how I got there and for a few horrible moments I thought I might have slept with her.

She rolled her eyes when I asked. "Not much use you were last night. Talk about brewer's droop, and babbling on about missing your wife too. I always pick the married ones! I should have left you in the bar."

I didn't bother correcting her. After all, I still feel married and being with another woman would feel like cheating. It doesn't get much worse – a drunk out looking for sympathy from strangers over his dead wife. I got out of that flat straight away and stumbled home. Talk about doing the walk of shame.

This is what rock bottom feels like. I've had enough. There's no point to it all. I'm not driving all the way to a cliff edge though, that's for sure. Bloody stupid idea that was. A bottle of whisky and a few packets of the right pills would probably do the job just fine. I've done a few searches on over-the-counter pills that are dangerous to mix with alcohol. All it would take is a trip to a couple of pharmacies to get enough pills. I wonder how long it would take to slip into a coma and how many pills I'd need. Is this really the way my world ends? Not with a bang but a whimper.

My phone buzzes. I hope it's not Steve. If I hear him tell me one more time that I shouldn't blame myself, I will scream.

It's not Steve. It's a message from an unknown number: 'John, check your email. Urgent. R'.

I can't believe my eyes for a moment. It can't be, but it looks like it is. He's been gone for weeks and now he picks this moment to contact me. I lie there staring at the ceiling, mulling over what to do. I always do what he tells me and where has that got me?

The compulsion is still there though. I open my email on my phone. Sixty-three unread messages. The most recent is titled 'Rooting for you'. It reads:

I'm worried about you, son of Adam.
You seem to have lost your bottle, or got lost in a bottle.
What happened? Cat got your tongue?
Trust your instincts and not your doubts,
Look back at the man with the 'crooked mouth'.

I throw the phone at the wall and shout, "Leave me alone!" I go to the window and yell it again. He's out there somewhere watching me, the sick bastard.

'Lost in a bottle'. He knows I've been drunk then. For all I know, he's been stalking me in bars, laughing at the mess I've become.

It takes me a while to calm down. Deep down, I think I knew he was still out there. The police might think they solved the Green Shoots case because the killings stopped when Abel Jackson was shot, but to me it just didn't fit. I bet he set up Jackson and used him the same way he's used me.

I pick up my phone and re-read the message. 'Cat got your tongue?' That's no coincidental turn of phrase. He doesn't do coincidences. That's his twisted sense of humour. He must be referring to Marcelo. He must know what happened, or maybe he even followed me there. It could have even been him that killed Marcelo. There was the cryptic note at the scene and the sadistic technique. Now he's turning his sadism back on me, teasing me with clues. Another bone thrown to the rabid dog.

I'm hungover as hell and in no state to deal with riddles. I take some painkillers, just two. I stare at the packet remembering what I was contemplating moments before and put the pills back in the bathroom cabinet.

I make some coffee to clear my head and open my computer. *Look back at the man with the 'crooked mouth'*. That could mean someone I've seen before, or I need to look into someone's past, or both.

'Crooked mouth' seems to be the main clue. I hadn't noticed at first but those two words are in quotation marks. I wonder why. I haven't met anyone in this investigation with a crooked mouth or a scar. It's more likely to be a metaphor, but anyone involved in this case is bound to be crooked, so that's too obvious.

I re-read the whole message. There's something else I missed. Why did he call me 'son of Adam'? There must be a reason. It reminds me of *The Lion, The Witch and The Wardrobe*, but that can't be it.

Son of Adam is the literal meaning of Adamson. Is that the clue? The literal meaning of a name? Maybe that's why 'crooked mouth' is in speech marks.

I go to a search engine and type it in. I don't find much, so I put in a few variations: 'origin crooked mouth' and 'name crooked mouth'.

And there it is: derived from Gaelic, crooked is 'cam' and mouth is 'beul'. 'Crooked mouth' is the literal meaning of a surname – Campbell.

Chapter 36

We were having a conversation that was on the brink of an argument. I admitted there was corruption in Britain but I thought it was nowhere near on the same scale as in Ecuador. You disagreed. I remember you responding: "How can you say that when most of the people in charge here went to the same damn school?"

I conceded the point but you wouldn't leave it there. "And what about the property market? That must be the biggest money laundering scheme in the world!"

Part of me wanted to argue, while another part of me agreed with you. "Maybe it is, but at least people can make the accusations you're making and publish them. The media regularly exposes corruption here. If journalists in Ecuador do that, they often end up dead."

You sighed. I held up my hands to indicate we should get off the subject and suggested a cup of tea. You laughed and gave me a hug. "Tea is the English answer to everything!"

After we had these discussions, I used to ask myself: are we just as bad in Britain? Do we really kid ourselves the system works? You used to say it was because Britain invented the colonial system, building an empire and syphoning off resources from poorer countries. I thought that was unfair and pointed out how much good Britain had done around the world. It was impossible not to get defensive about my country.

My limited experience of Ecuador has shown me that nobody kids themselves about the widespread corruption. Most people there have a fatalistic view – '*así es la vida*' ('that's life'). You always said that fatalism annoyed you. It didn't surprise me people reacted like that though. Maybe it's just easier not to care, especially if caring can be dangerous.

I'm reminded of these conversations as I try to piece together this jigsaw. I went to Ecuador to investigate crime and corruption but maybe I've overlooked the corruption on my own doorstep. Root, my friendly neighbourhood psychopath stalker, has thrown me another clue – that I should look into Campbell and look into his past, so maybe I will find the answers in London after all.

I do a few searches for his company and he has a website. He told me he worked mainly in agricultural exports. His client list includes a banana company, chocolate and flowers. I scroll through the list one by one until I come to AUSUK Inc. I click on the company website. It's an Anglo-Australian mining company. I look through the company's news pages and there's an announcement of a new project in Ecuador, accompanied by a photo. It's hard to pinpoint the exact location but it's next to a river in a forest. It looks similar to the area I've just visited, where Christina was researching. Campbell never mentioned he worked with mining clients. I wonder what else he didn't mention.

According to the biography page on his website, Campbell is an engineer. He has 'Cantab' after his name so he must have studied at Cambridge. I do a few more searches online. I don't find much but there are some photos from a birthday party – Campbell's 50th. It's dated two years ago, so I deduce he probably studied at Cambridge over 30 years ago.

I look online for the Cambridge Alumni Association and get a contact number. It's time for a bit of acting so I put on my best middle-aged upper-class voice. "Good morning. Is that the Alumni Association? Excellent. I'm wondering if you could help me. We're having a bit of a get-together this week with some old pals from Cambridge and I'm trying to locate one of my former classmates. Yes, his name is Charles Campbell. I'm hazy on exactly which year he graduated, but I'd put it somewhere around 1988 or '89 I think."

The lady on the line is happy to help. "I can certainly look him up for you but I can't give out any details before getting Mr Campbell's permission. We could forward correspondence though."

"I understand, of course. Could you see if you can find contact details and I could send an email for you to forward? Then it's up to Charles if he would like to attend. It's the day after tomorrow you see, hence the hurry. I'm awfully sorry."

She puts me on hold for a few minutes while she looks at the database, then comes back on the line. "There are a few Campbells but the only man of that name who was at the university in the late 1980s is an Anthony Campbell. Oh yes – Anthony Charles Campbell. Perhaps he uses his middle name?"

"That's the only one you have? He's in London now, I believe."

She hesitates. "Well, I shouldn't really give out that information, but yes there is a forwarding address in London. I suggest you send an email to the association and I will forward it on." She dictates the address and I hang up.

Anthony Charles Campbell – there's something familiar about that. I look back through my notes from Ecuador. The foreigner Christina mentioned, a tall man named 'Tonio'. Campbell is a tall foreigner and his first name is Anthony. That would be 'Antonio' in Spanish. Jesus, it must be him. Tonio is Campbell. It's been staring me in the face the whole time.

This would explain everything. He wanted the Jaguarcocha community forced off their land so mining could begin. It would explain why he was there at the hospital. He must have been involved in the forged diagnosis. That's why he was so helpful and so persuasive about arranging a quick cremation. I've been such a fool.

246

I punch the wall in frustration. It bloody hurts. A broken hand isn't going to help me. I need to think about what to do next. If Campbell was involved in Christina's death, then I have to go after him, but proving it will be a tough prospect. Nina hadn't actually met him. Marcelo had a vague description but he wasn't sure, and even if he were, he's dead now.

The reality is I've got nothing that would stand up in court. I was chased out of Ecuador before I could gather more details of who Marcelo met. I can't ask Richie to follow it up either because he's staying out of the case for his own safety. That leaves me with no option other than to confront Campbell and try to get him to incriminate himself. It's a long shot, but I could pull out a few tricks and pretend I have more evidence than I actually do.

I may as well try the direct approach, so I call Campbell's office. It's the same frosty receptionist from last time. She barely masks her disdain upon hearing my name. It's no surprise to be told Campbell is unavailable. Booked up all week and due to travel next week. A likely story. I tell her to inform Campbell to expect an urgent email. I go back to my computer and type it out.

Dear Mr 'Tonio' Campbell,

I'm writing to inform you of the results of my recent investigations into the death of my wife Christina. I have collected testimony from several witnesses that lead me to conclude without doubt that my wife was poisoned along with four community leaders in Jaguarcocha, Ecuador.

I have testimony that the diagnosis of dengue fever and results of the autopsy were fabricated at Clinica Interamericana in Quito. I also have evidence and eye-witness statements that show the poisoning was arranged by an intermediary for a mining company with which you have close connections. Only now do I understand the real reasons you were at the hospital when my wife died.

The weight of the evidence shows you were involved in the crime and I intend to publish my findings. However, I will first extend you the opportunity to meet me to explain your actions and offer your side of the story before I go public. You have 48 hours to respond.

John Bautista Adamson

If he calls my bluff, I'm short of options, but I'll cross that bridge if I come to it. I know the newspaper won't even touch this, and I have nothing that would stand up in court or defend me from a lawsuit. Campbell doesn't know all that though. I'll have to see if he takes the bait.

Chapter 37: Campbell

Charles Campbell phoned reception to say he was not to be disturbed for the rest of the morning. This email from John Adamson was unexpected, although from everything he'd heard about him, it wasn't entirely surprising he would go so far.

'Evidence and witness statements' – Campbell doubted that was true, but it was still a serious concern. A man like this with nothing to lose could cause a lot of damage. Meeting him could be risky too.

Campbell's phone vibrated – another call from a withheld number. It was the second time in a few minutes. Campbell ignored it again, but then a message appeared: 'Answer the phone, Mr Campbell. You have a journalist problem we can solve'.

That got Campbell's attention. Whoever sent the message must know about Adamson. The phone rang again and this time Campbell answered it.

"Mr Campbell?"

"To whom am I speaking?"

"Who I am is unimportant. It's what I know and what

I can do for you that matters."

"That's a bit cloak and dagger, isn't it? But you've got my attention – get to the point."

"We know you've been contacted by a certain journalist – a troublesome, persistent man. It so happens we have a shared interest in dealing with this individual. I represent clients and he has become a thorn in their side, a thorn which needs to be... removed."

"I see. Can I ask how you came by this information?"

"We've been keeping a close eye on this man for some time on behalf of our clients."

"Right. I agree he is definitely troublesome. I had hoped he would see reason and no further action would be necessary. I haven't agreed to meet him yet. My lawyer advises against it and I'm currently seeking an injunction to stop any publication of falsehoods."

"That sounds wise, but the internet is a difficult place to police, Mr Campbell. Even if an injunction works with national media, there is plenty of damage he could do through other sources."

"True. What course of action do your clients wish to take then?"

"Let's not spell that out over the phone, but suffice to say he needs to be dealt with decisively and permanently. His request for a meeting with you presents a fortuitous opportunity for us both. We would like you to meet him at a designated place at a designated time. We will do the rest."

Campbell sighed. "I hope you will have better luck

with this than my associates in Ecuador. The whole episode is regrettable but perhaps it would be a kindness, considering what he has endured."

"Yes, a kindness. Now, listen carefully, Mr Campbell. There is a private members' club called The Maximón in Bloomsbury."

"Yes, that rings a bell."

"We will arrange for you to have a private room at the back of the club tomorrow at six p.m. An associate of mine, Miss Gonzalez, will arrive shortly afterwards. You will say she is your lawyer. She will take care of business and take Mr Adamson to a more private meeting."

"You're sending a woman?"

"Yes. Do not concern yourself, Mr Campbell. I assure you she is vastly experienced."

"Okay. Agreed then. I will make the arrangements. It will be a relief to close this matter. I hope I will not hear from you again."

The man on the line chuckled softly. "Oh, don't worry, Mr Campbell. Our business concludes tomorrow. Goodbye."

Chapter 38

Dear Mr Adamson,

Following receipt of your email yesterday, please be advised I have sought an injunction against the publication of the falsehoods you mention.

I wish to bring this matter to a close, so I will meet you – and you alone – tomorrow at 6 p.m. at The Maximón club in Bloomsbury. There is a private room booked under my name.

Charles Campbell

I'm a little surprised to receive this reply as I'd half-expected to be ignored completely by Campbell. His threat of an injunction is expected though. It's a moot point as no editor would touch this story for lack of verifiable evidence. My only tactic is to pretend I have more evidence than I do. It's a long shot, I know. Regardless, I want to look Campbell in the eye and tell him I know he was behind my wife's death, and I won't let up until he pays for the crime.

I don't know The Maximón club. In my experience,

private members' clubs are filled with the most insufferable people – old money of landed gentry mixing uncomfortably with new money keen to show off their wealth. Definitely not my scene.

The club is quiet so early in the evening. No doubt Campbell wants it that way. A few elderly men in suits regard me disapprovingly. I'm underdressed of course. This is no special occasion and I'm certainly not dressing formally for Campbell. I talk to the receptionist, who confirms the booking of the Green Room at the back.

The room is opulently decorated with light green mosaic, a dark green leather sofa, deep green carpet and an oblong mahogany table at the centre, with Campbell sitting at the head. He's predictable, I'll give him that. He's trying to let me know he's in charge and this is his meeting to which I've been invited.

"Mr Adamson, take a seat. Would you like a drink or something to eat perhaps? I'm told the food here is excellent, although I dined earlier."

He looks relaxed, as if none of this troubles him, which only annoys me even more.

"I'm not here to break bread with you, Mr Campbell, as you well know."

"No, well I'm merely being polite, but let's get to the heart of the matter then, shall we? I must say, I was taken aback by your email and your preposterous allegations. Perhaps you can enlighten me as to how you came to such erroneous conclusions?"

"Not erroneous at all, Mr Campbell. I have a source at the hospital, who confirmed the fabrication of the diagnosis that my wife had dengue fever. It was due to pressure from above. I have no doubt that explains your presence at the hospital."

"Good god, Mr Adamson. I was trying to help a British citizen. And I did help, did I not?"

"Oh yes, you were very keen to rush through a cremation, making the true cause of death impossible to verify. Very clever. I should never have agreed to it."

Campbell shakes his head in amazement. "Preposterous. With enough money, you can get people to say anything in Ecuador. Who gave you this false information?"

"I'm not telling you that. I have no doubt it would put them in danger. I have a lot more evidence. The symptoms were consistent with poisoning, according to my source. Furthermore, a former member of the Jaguarcocha community admits he was threatened by a man and given a toxin with instructions to give it to the leaders at a meeting. He identified you as working with this man. This meeting in Jaguarcocha was convened to decide how to resist a mining company – AUSUK, a company you work with. It's well-documented on your website and the company's website."

"Is that all you have? Some Indian's claims? Yes, I work with mining companies along with many other companies. That is not a crime."

"He identified you from a photograph as the man

who gave the orders. I believe you use your first name Anthony, abbreviated to Tonio. You are well-known by that name in Lago Agrio."

Campbell raises his eyebrows at this. I can see I've rattled him. I'm lying of course. Marcelo never clearly identified him, but he doesn't know that.

It's getting very hot in here. There seems to be heat blasting through the walls, unnecessary on a warm April day. I'm starting to sweat, so I take off my jacket.

There's a knock at the door. A woman with red hair dressed in a trouser suit arrives, bringing a jug of water and glasses.

Campbell looks pleased. "Ah, good evening, Miss Gonzalez. Mr Adamson, this is one of my legal advisers. She will join us to observe that nothing gets out of hand."

The woman nods at me and sets down the jug and glasses, which is of some relief because the heat is making me thirsty.

"Now, where were we, Mr Adamson? Oh yes, the Jaguarcocha community. Your wild allegations are very wide of the mark. The facts are these: sometimes it's necessary to negotiate with local communities, who are generously compensated for providing access, but nobody is threatened and certainly not poisoned on behalf of clients. Aside from it being an unspeakable crime, it's simply not a good way to do business. We are in the business of making the most of opportunities. Ecuador is rich in natural resources and these types of investments help lift millions in the country out of poverty. Would you prefer they ran around in loincloths with blowguns? This is the twenty-first century!"

He gives a hollow laugh.

"Your prejudices are very obvious, Mr Campbell, as are your lies. I believe you did all you could to remove a community you saw as an inconvenient obstacle."

"Ridiculous. Is this person who claims to identify me willing to testify to that? I doubt it would stand up in court."

"As you probably know, Mr Campbell, the man is dead. He was murdered in Quito. Not a coincidence, I'm sure."

"Good god. If I heard you right, are you now accusing me of committing even more crimes? The idea I would sanction any murder is utterly false, and libellous, Mr Adamson. I won't stand for it. I am guilty of nothing more than conducting business."

"You are certainly guilty, Mr Campbell. Proving it is another matter, but I won't stop until I do. There's nothing noble about destroying communities and forests that have existed for generations."

I'm starting to feel woozy. I drink some more water. It's so hot in this room. I notice the woman is watching me closely.

She says, "You don't look very well, Mr Adamson. Perhaps you need some air?"

I try to stand, but I'm unsteady on my feet. She takes me by the arm. "Mr Campbell, would you mind helping me take Mr Adamson outside? He's not feeling very well."

I hear Campbell say, "Yes, I think it's best we draw our meeting to a close now. I have nothing further to say. I admit I'm not feeling particularly good myself."

She leads me down a corridor and out through an exit. I think Campbell is following behind. They must have drugged me. I've walked straight into a trap. I have no strength to resist as I'm put into a car.

"Hello, John. Nice to see you again."

The voice is familiar.

Chapter 39

Till human voices wake us, and we drown.

I drift in and out of consciousness. I don't know where I am. I open my eyes and in front of me is a steering wheel. I'm still in a car but I seem to be in the driver's seat.

The wind is howling outside. There's a faint light on the horizon. I'm groggy but I think I'm on the coast. It must be either past sunset or nearly sunrise, I can't tell. I don't know how long I was out. I try to move but it's difficult.

This feels familiar. I think I'm close to a cliff edge. I look to my left to see a man in the passenger seat with his head turned away from me. It's Campbell. He appears to be asleep.

"Welcome back, John."

I flinch and try to turn. The voice comes from behind me in the back seat.

"Look in the rear-view mirror, John. Easier to talk that way."

I recognise the voice, that accent that's hard to place.

He sounds like the man on the phone who called himself Root.

"You remember me from our correspondence, John. And of course, we have met once before."

I look closer at him in the mirror – thick dark hair, broad shoulders. I realise I have met him. He's the man who saved us in Quito.

He smiles as the realisation dawns. "Don't I get a thank you, John? This may be the third time I've saved your life."

I remember I was in a room with Campbell. There was a woman, then I started feeling drowsy. I must have blacked out. There's nobody else in the car, so it seems she's already played her part.

"Saving my life, is that what you're doing? I presume it was your associate who drugged me."

"Sorry about that, John, but it was the best way for us to have time to talk, and also to give you a chance for justice."

He glances at Campbell. I'm guessing he's also been drugged.

"So, we're next on your list?"

"Not you, John, but let's see how things play out. The man next to you is much more a model target. You know he's guilty better than anyone."

So he plans to kill Campbell. I despise the man, but that's not what I want.

"While you're thinking about that, John, let's talk. You're the journalist so you must have a lot of questions. This would be quite a scoop, although I insist that nothing we discuss here be disclosed. As you know, I'm not a man to cross. But for personal curiosity at least, by all means fire away."

He's right. I do have questions.

"How did you know where I was that night at Beachy Head?"

"Good question, John. I'll respond with one of my own. How do the police track people?"

I consider it for a moment. "Traffic cameras, transactions, logins, phone location."

He raises his eyebrows at my last guess. My phone then. How could that be? I remember my phone was missing for a few days back in February before I found it in the car. I think it was the week before I was on the cliffs. It must have been him. He's been tracking me even longer than I realised.

"It's amazing how much information can be gleaned from a phone, John. It's a strategy that has served me well, and served you well too on that particular night. I've often wondered if you would have pressed the accelerator if the police hadn't arrived."

I don't know the answer to that.

"Okay, sensitive subject. Let's leave it. You must have more questions."

"How did you know so much about Christina, and about Campbell?"

"I've spent a lot of time in South America and keep a close eye on things there. Those leaders who died were well-known locally. The Western media usually ignores such news stories but it made Latin American news. Campbell has been on my radar for some time and, as I said, it's amazing how much information a person keeps on their phone and email."

Now I recall Campbell mentioned an email crash and the loss of his phone when I first saw him in London. Most of the victims lost their phones shortly before they were killed. This must be his *modus operandi*.

"I have a question of my own, John. Tell me, back in Quito, how did you feel when you found Marcelo dead?"

I wasn't expecting that question, but then he's rarely predictable.

"I felt nothing, except revulsion at the way he was killed."

"Oh, come on, John. Don't lie to me. Tell me how it really made you feel."

I remember what Steve said to me afterwards, that I looked almost happy about it. It was uncomfortable to hear.

"Some relief in a way. I hated him, but when I saw him dead that hatred was gone."

"Ah yes, the peace that comes with closure and with justice served. I know it well. Marcelo did long for peace, I could see it in his eyes."

He looks at me intently. He's waiting for another realisation to dawn. My instincts were right then. He wasn't only there to save us from being shot. It was him who killed Marcelo.

"I thought it might be you."

"I just helped the process along, John. He didn't need much persuasion. But he got a little tongue-tied in the end, so it was hard to tell what he wanted."

That sick sense of humour. I feel nauseous just thinking about it.

"As I said, John, you should be thanking me for that night. And tonight, your vengeance will be complete."

"I don't want that type of vengeance. I'm not like you. I want Campbell to face justice in court, in prison."

"That's naïve and you know it. This man will never see the inside of a courtroom or a prison cell. You don't have enough evidence, a key witness is dead and his pockets are very deep."

I know he's right. I'm clutching at straws hoping Campbell would incriminate himself.

"But there are other ways to fight than murder."

He snorts. "There may be other ways, but I find them unreliable. Use the justice system and they buy off judges and threaten witnesses. Protest in the street and the authorities intimidate, even criminalising peaceful protest in London. Try to use democracy, then the elite fix elections and buy off the media. And if by some miracle the right people do win elections, what happens? Just ask the Kennedy family, or the Roldós family in Ecuador."

"You really think it's justice to pick off oil, timber and beef executives? Where does it end? Are you going to target consumers who buy those products next?"

"Now there's an idea, John, but no. I prefer to target the perpetrators and dish out my own justice. As you know, they are killed by the very thing they prize the most.

"You're a TS Eliot fan, aren't you, John? 'I will show you fear in a handful of dust' – I'm fond of that line, but overall I like the romantics more. Shelley, Blake, and a particular favourite is Wordsworth."

He starts to recite, staring out the window as he does so.

"Sweet is the lore which nature brings;
Our meddling intellect
Misshapes the beauteous forms of things:–
We murder to dissect."

He smiles at the word 'murder'.

"*The Tables Turned* the poem is called. That's what I'm doing, John – turning the tables. I wonder if you've heard the story of the Jivaro tribe in Ecuador. No? It's a good one. Back in the sixteenth century, the Spanish took over Jivaro territory, fuelled by their thirst for gold. But the Jivaro attacked the town of Logroño and captured the Spanish governor. They executed him by pouring molten gold down his throat until his insides burst, thus fulfilling his thirst for gold. Now that is justice. I tried a variation of it on your colleague Rupert."

I flinch at the image. I wonder if he's deliberately baiting me. "You think someone deserves to die for expressing an opinion you don't like? What did killing him achieve? There are many others to write similar blogs. It won't stop corporations ravaging the Amazon basin either, that's for sure."

"How can you be so sure? You need to look deeper."

"What do you mean?"

"I'm not going into details now, John, but as I said, it's amazing how much information can be accessed with the right tools. Access to corporate accounts is easier when they operate on the fringes of the law. I work with people who have a particularly useful and lucrative set of skills."

"Is that why some of the victims were kept alive for several days? You were getting what you needed to steal from their companies?"

"You're quick, John. That's not all though. I also work with partners who know the markets. Have you any idea how much money can be made with the right information to trade at the right time when an industry comes under attack? Let's say, for example, a person were to sell stocks just before a plunge caused by unforeseen events, then buy at the bottom of the market and wait until the authorities catch those responsible, causing the stocks to rocket again. The profits could stretch to eight figures, even nine."

"Insider trading and hacking? So you're just a thief. This was all about money?"

"Of course it's about money, John. Why do corporations kill and plunder? For money. To fight them, we need money."

"Money for more killing?"

"No, money to defend the Earth. Security needs paying, judges need paying, and investment is necessary to boost the right type of growth. You'll see what I mean in time. The greatest battle of this century is between extractionists and ecologists. Pick a side, John. Capitalism has created a post-moral world. It's not called the rat race for nothing – the winners are the biggest rats. Making money is not a philosophy, it's not a moral choice, haven't you noticed?"

"Maybe, but if you use the same brutal tactics, you're no better than them."

"It's not about how we get there, but where we end up, John. Imagine if we eliminated the richest one per cent that owns half the world's wealth, then redistributed it all. Wouldn't that be a worthy cause?"

"You're talking about killing seventy million people!"

"Hypothetically, but that one per cent has the rest of humanity in a chokehold. You don't loosen a chokehold with words; you do it by force."

He clenches his fist. He's starting to look agitated so I decide not to argue further. He's not a man I want to anger.

He continues. "If we don't change course, it will be out of the ashes of the human race that green shoots will grow. Mankind has declared war on the Earth and the Earth is fighting back. Have you ever been to

Chernobyl, John? Do you know that in just thirty years it became a city of trees and wild animals? Humans are terrified of radiation, but life goes on for other species, with or without us.

"We live in a world run by psychopaths who hold nothing sacred but the god money. How many do governments and corporations kill? Hundreds, thousands every year, including your wife. The West doesn't bother to count casualties because they're mainly from the third world. It's about time there was pushback."

"But what about Abel Jackson? He was an activist. Did he deserve what happened to him? You set him up good and proper. Was that justice?"

"Now you're asking the tough questions, John. Good. That was regrettable, but for every action there is a reaction, and what a reaction there was to his death. He would have been proud of the part he played."

"I'm sure he'd have preferred to live."

"If killing Abel makes me Cain, the first man to raise his arm in anger, I'm fine with that."

I see headlights behind me in the distance. I don't know exactly where we are but it crosses my mind there might be a police patrol.

"I see you may be wondering if the police might come and get you again, John. Don't worry, I picked a quieter spot down the coast. I wouldn't want us to be disturbed."

So much for that idea. I have one more question for

266

him.

"Why me? Why did you choose me?"

"Ah, now there's a question."

He looks out the window. For a moment, I see a flicker of emotion on his face.

"We have more in common than you know, John. You may find it hard to believe, but a long time ago there was someone precious to me. Like you, I lost her to evil men. Like you, I thought of dying, but I found vengeance a powerful motivator. I felt a strong affinity towards you because we had something terrible in common. Even your name seemed to fit. John Bautista Adamson – John the Baptist, son of Adam."

I look at him in disbelief. "Now you're really sounding crazy. If I'm John the Baptist, do you have a messiah complex?"

"No, I have too much of the devil in me for that, and I prefer the Old Testament to the New anyway – the vengeful god who gets things done.

"You may wonder why I brought you back to a cliff edge. Think of it as a metaphor, if you will. This is where the human race has led us. Men like Campbell would have us drive over it in pursuit of money. It's only fitting he experiences that journey literally."

So that's how he plans to kill Campbell. I'm wondering if he intends me to join him.

"If you want to send Campbell over a cliff, why do you need me?"

"Who said I would do it? It's obvious, John, surely?

You're in the driving seat."

"You want me to drive off a cliff and die with him?"

"I stopped you from doing that once before, John. No, that wouldn't be my first choice. Better if you just press the gas and jump out. I've brought something along to make it easier."

He holds up a brick. I'm guessing he wants me to jam it on the accelerator.

"That's your plan? For me to do your dirty work?"

"I can see you have doubts. Perhaps you need a little persuasion."

He reaches in his jacket pocket, takes out a phone and presses a button. It's a recording. I recognise the voices – it's him and Campbell talking. Campbell says, "I hope you will have better luck than my associates in Ecuador. This whole episode is regrettable but perhaps it would be a kindness, considering what he has endured."

He stops the recording. "Charles Campbell showing his true colours. Tell me, would getting rid of you be a kindness, John? I don't think so. I think you have much more to give. Better the guilty man dies and the good man lives. It would complete justice for Christina. After all, if it weren't for this man, she'd be alive, John."

I look at Campbell and hesitate for a moment. He may be right, but this is not who I am. If I cross that line, I will never come back. I'm not doing it.

"Even if that's true, I'm a writer. I'm no killer."

He looks at me for a long time, then shakes his head. He's disappointed.

"No, you are neither. You are an errand boy sent by grocery clerks to collect the bill."

It takes me a moment to recognise the reference – Colonel Kurtz in *Apocalypse Now*.

I shake my head and stare back at him. "Are you as crazy as Kurtz, then?"

"Be careful, John. I may have the heart of darkness but I know exactly what I'm doing. If you're not on my side, John, are you on his?"

He nods at Campbell, who is beginning to murmur. He's waking up.

"We are the dead, John. They will get us in the end. It's just a question of when and where, but I'm not done yet, not by a long shot. You are though, John. This is where we say goodbye."

I feel a sharp pain on the back of my head. The light on the horizon fades.

Chapter 40: Campbell

He needed to move fast. Campbell was waking up and he wanted him to be semi-conscious for this. Fully conscious and it could be difficult to pull off, but unconscious and Campbell would miss the entire show. He didn't want that.

It was a pity about John. He dragged him out the car and left him on the grass a few metres away.

He wiped down the seats, steering wheel and dashboard. He couldn't assume DNA would be destroyed by the fall. He got into the driving seat and switched on the engine. It was far from easy and had to be done exactly the right way.

Campbell was moaning, slowly recovering consciousness. He'd been given more sedative than John and apparently had a full stomach from dinner so the effects were lasting longer.

He reached in Campbell's inside pocket for his phone and texted a single word: 'Rocks'. He smiled. Everything was as it should be.

He then reached across Campbell to lock the

passenger door. He wouldn't want him to jump out, although that looked unlikely unless Campbell came round very quickly.

He shifted the car into gear but kept the handbrake on. He jammed the brick against the accelerator and the car revved loudly. It was an expensive car – a man like Campbell drove a top-of-the-range brand of course. He smiled at how fitting it was that Campbell would die in a machine named Jaguar. The forest gods would appreciate the offering.

Campbell opened and closed his eyes, mumbling something incoherent. He opened the driver's door slightly and readied himself. He had to take off Campbell's seat belt. It would guarantee his death but also help ensure it would be ruled suicide, not foul play. After all, nobody drives off a cliff voluntarily while strapped in the passenger seat.

He patted Campbell on the shoulder. "Well, Charles, it's only fitting for a man who has made a killing from rocks that you spend your final seconds hurtling towards them. This is for Jaguarcocha and for Christina Bautista Adamson."

Campbell opened his eyes and looked around in confusion. He flicked Campbell's seatbelt off, then released the handbrake and the car shot forwards. He jumped out of the driver's door and rolled on the grass, stopping just a few metres from the edge of the cliff.

The car powered forwards. Campbell was not sure if it was a nightmare or real as the ground disappeared.

The car floated for a split second, then plunged.

Campbell hit the windscreen and caught a glimpse of the white rocks emerging from the twilight below. He opened his mouth to cry out before the impact crushed the life from his body.

Chapter 41

I'm not sure if I'm alive or dead. My head hurts like hell, I know that much, and I have grass in my mouth, so either I'm alive or the afterlife is very disappointing.

It's dark. I must have been out for a while. I look around to try to get my bearings. The black void in front of me is familiar. I'm still on the cliff edge, around ten or twenty metres back. He must have dragged me out of the car and left me on the grass.

I try to stand but I'm still groggy. I crawl over to where I think the car was parked and feel the ground. I look to my right towards the cliff edge and see tyre tracks have churned up the grass.

I crawl towards the cliff, following the tracks. They lead all the way to the edge. I stop a couple of metres back. I guess this means Campbell is dead. Root must have leapt out. I can't imagine he went over too.

I look at the ground and see patches where the grass is flattened. Looking down the slope, a few footprints are barely visible. He must be long gone.

I stand up and turn to face the cliff edge. I step

forward. I'm barely two metres from the edge. A gust of wind hits me, pushing me forward, and I instinctively step back again. If I go any closer to the edge to search for the car, I might get blown over.

All it would take is a rush of blood to lunge forward and I'd be gone in seconds. I wonder if it would be quick. I've read of jumpers who weren't killed by the fall but lay in agony for hours. I've even read of people who landed on a ledge and survived. I step back from the edge. This is not how I want my story to end.

In the distance, I can see lights, so I make my way slowly down the hill towards them. It will be a relief to get away from this bleak place.

As I approach the lights, I recognise where I am. Then I see a sign. It's Birling Gap, a tiny beach village where the cliffs dip down between Beachy Head and the Seven Sisters. So I must have been on the Seven Sisters. Root was right about one thing: we weren't disturbed by the police, unfortunately for Campbell.

My throat is dry and I'm suddenly aware of being very thirsty. I can't have drunk anything since I was drugged hours ago. As I reach Birling Gap, most of the houses are dark. It must be well after midnight. I don't want to disturb anyone, particularly as I don't want to be connected to what happened to Campbell.

I see a staircase down to the beach. Nearby is a basin and taps. I hurry towards it and cup my hands, drinking and drinking. It's the sweetest water I've ever tasted.

I wonder whether I should phone a taxi and go home,

but something makes me want to linger here longer. I walk down the iron staircase and sit on the pebble beach. It's so peaceful in the light of a half moon. I wonder if it's waxing or waning. I like to think it's waxing.

I wonder what time it is and reach in my inside pocket for my phone. As I take it out, a piece of paper falls from the phone case. It's a handwritten note.

Dear John,

Hope your head's not too sore. Sorry but it was necessary.

If you're reading this, I hope you've decided to live. I'm glad. I didn't mean what I said – you are no errand boy. I have no illusions about who I am, but you are one of the good ones.

You can be proud of what you've done and be proud of your wife. The world needs people like you.

I won't disturb you any further, provided you do not disturb me.

R

I re-read it. I see the irony of a mass murderer paying me compliments, but as always with him, there's a sting in the tail – a clear warning to leave him alone. I'm happy to do so. I don't want to end up like the others and I've solved Christina's case now, which was the only reason to maintain contact with him.

I think I'll leave phoning that taxi until morning. I want to stay on the beach and watch the sunrise. I remember the last time we did this together. I was having a tough time at work and, as usual, I was bringing the stress home. We went on holiday to Thailand and one night we stayed up and watched the sunrise on the beach. It was so beautiful, it brought tears to your eyes. I put my arm around you and I remember you told me something your dad used to say: "Even in the middle of the darkest night, remember the sun always rises in the morning."

I must have nodded off because the next thing I see is light emerging in the east. As the sun peaks over the horizon, I know you're willing me on to keep going. If that's what you want, then that's what I'll do.

I want to live.

Chapter 42: Plata

Jorge Plata had been a judge in Ecuador for over three years. He remembered clearly the day he arrived at the law courts for his interview for the role. It was a very proud day for him. He was the first man in his family to become a qualified lawyer, and after 15 years in the profession, it was an honour to be considered for such a distinguished post. It was also a day when his eyes opened, and he would never again be under any illusions about how the system worked.

His interview had gone quite well with questions from a panel of three judges about his experience and some legal scenarios to discuss. He was delighted and surprised that they offered him the position immediately.

Then things became more difficult. The panel informed him that the 'administration and certification fees' to become a judge would cost $100,000. He could either pay that amount himself or take the option of discussing a 'grant' from a consortium, an option the panel recommended. At this point, the panellists left the room and a group of men arrived. They neither smiled nor shook his hand. Their demeanour made him uncomfortable.

One of the men, who appeared to be in charge, explained that their 'consortium' would be pleased to pay Jorge's fees on condition that he consulted with them on certain cases. The man emphasised this 'consultation' was a mandatory part of the agreement and breaking it would have severe consequences. Something about the way he said those last words made Jorge's blood run cold.

Jorge thought it through after the men left the room, but he could see no alternative. He didn't have the money to pay the fees himself, so he could either stay as a mere lawyer or accept their terms.

He agreed to the deal and went home to tell his wife Pilar he'd got the job. His family was delighted. Pilar threw him a surprise party that weekend, but even she noticed he wasn't really enjoying himself. He didn't seem as happy about his promotion as she'd expected.

Over three years, Jorge Plata did not put a foot wrong with his paymasters. The consortium would instruct him on the best course of action for particular cases and he would rule accordingly. Jorge noticed they were particularly active on drugs cases, but also on a range of civil suits, usually involving large corporations.

After a while, he became accustomed to a more luxurious lifestyle than he'd ever dreamed possible, and his huge house and domestic staff helped alleviate his initial unease at the arrangement.

This latest case had troubled Judge Plata though. The plaintiffs were a group of indigenous families from a remote jungle village named Jaguarcocha. They were suing a mining company for destruction and pollution of their land. Their lawyer was a bilingual American named Maria Carmen de la Cruz, who had proven highly efficient at building a strong case. She produced an extensive portfolio of evidence, including scientifically analysed samples of the water supply and medical details of birth defects among the community children, attributed to mercury poisoning.

The leader of the plaintiffs was a young widowed mother of three named Nina. She spoke with great conviction and dignity about what her community had suffered, including the unexplained death of her husband. Judge Plata knew exactly what 'unexplained' really meant. He'd seen so many key witnesses and plaintiffs disappear in mysterious circumstances during the past three years.

Jorge was contacted early on by the consortium. He was instructed that the mining company had a strong defence and the plaintiffs' case had no merit. The verdict must be clear and decisive, he was told.

On the morning he was due to give his verdict, his wife and his two children, Jorgito and Rafaela, left the house early for school in the far north of Quito. The court session in the centre of the city did not start until midday so he had plenty of time. By nine a.m., his wife had not returned from school, but he guessed she had probably gone to the mall or the hair salon.

He took a shower and got dressed in the bathroom before returning to the master bedroom to fetch his tie and jacket. As he entered the room, there was a man sitting on the bed. He pointed a gun with a silencer at Jorge.

"Close the door, Judge Plata, and hand me your cell phone."

The man spoke in Spanish, but with a foreign accent. He was big and towered over Jorge when he stood up to take his phone.

Jorge's mind was racing. He wondered how this man had got past the security gates. He had no idea what he'd done wrong either. He was fulfilling his side of the deal with the consortium.

The man scrolled through Jorge's phone. "Pilar – this is your wife's number, correct? My partners met her and your two beautiful children earlier this morning. They've taken a detour from school. I'm sure their teachers will understand, so don't worry. You should talk to your wife now."

The man held up the phone on speaker. Jorge's wife was crying and wailing: "Please don't hurt my babies!"

Jorge said, "Pilar, are you okay? And the children?"

"Yes, we're not hurt, but I'm scared, Jorge…"

The man hung up the phone before Pilar could say any more.

Jorge felt his world collapsing. This man had his

280

family, his entire world.

"What do you want? I've always done as the consortium asks. You must know that."

"I imagine you have Jorge, but this Jaguarcocha case is particularly important to me."

"I've agreed to side with the defence and dismiss it. What more do you want?"

"Ah Jorge, I see that you have looked at the evidence in front of you and come to the wrong conclusion. I do not work for this consortium you mention. I make my own decisions. You should try it some time, it's very liberating."

"I don't understand. Please tell me what you want. Don't hurt my family."

"Don't look so sad, Jorge. You have an opportunity to do a great thing today. You can save your family and you can deliver the right verdict in court too. It's a win-win."

Jorge frowned. "What do you mean 'the right verdict'?"

"You are aware the Jaguarcocha community has a strong case, correct?"

Jorge hesitated. He didn't know what the correct answer would be. He nodded.

"Well, all you have to do to save your family is to side with the plaintiffs and award compensation of this amount to the community." The man showed Jorge a piece of paper.

"I cannot do that. The consortium will kill me!"

281

"They may try, but not if they cannot find you. I on the other hand have already found you. I may not kill you, but your family will certainly die – little Rafaela first, next Jorgito, then finally your wife Pilar, after my partners have enjoyed her of course. I think it might be a worse punishment to let you live rather than kill you, knowing you could have saved them all."

Jorge put his head in his hands.

"All of this will happen, Jorge, unless you do as I say."

Jorge saw no way out. He had to get his family safe, even if it meant the consortium would kill him.

"Okay."

"Okay what? Repeat what you will do today in court."

"I will award the case to the plaintiffs and set compensation at the amount you showed me."

"Good, and make it a convincing verdict, Jorge. That is important. Make it reflect the strength of the case and the guilt of the mining company. We will be in the courtroom listening. As soon as the verdict is confirmed, you will go to the back exit of the courthouse and a car will take you to your family. I advise you to go straight to the airport. As a gesture of goodwill, I have opened a bank account in your name in Panama. There will be funds transferred when you have completed your side of the bargain, so you will not need to return to Ecuador. Are we clear, Jorge?"

Jorge nodded.

282

"Stay in this room for fifteen minutes while I leave and do not contact your wife until after delivering the verdict or the deal is off, is that understood?"

Jorge nodded. After the man left, he lay on the bed shaking. He realised he needed to compose a completely different statement for the court session. Knowing his family's lives depended on it, he sat down at his desk to write out a draft.

An hour later, Judge Jorge Plata drove to the courthouse and parked in his usual space at the back. As he exited the car, he was startled to see the side wall of the courthouse had been painted with an enormous mural. It was a scene of ashes and death on one side with trees, animals and children on the other. Under the painting, in white paint, it read: '*De sus cenizas, crecerán brotes verdes*'. Jorge stared at it. He found the artwork strangely comforting. There was hope he would see his family again.

As Judge Plata read out his verdict, there were gasps throughout the courtroom. He found the mining company guilty of negligence resulting in the destruction of the community and lifelong impact on their health. The company was ordered to pay $10 million. Jorge made brief eye contact with a man at the back of the court, a man who a few hours previously had pointed a gun at him in his bedroom. The man nodded at him curtly and left, while Judge Plata made a swift exit out the back, ignoring the pleas of the mining company's lawyers, who were incandescent with rage.

The lawyer Maria Carmen de la Cruz beamed with pride and hugged Nina, who was weeping and cradling her youngest child. Neither of them had dared to expect this. They exited the courthouse and were surrounded by reporters asking for their reaction to the judgement.

Nina said, "I will never get my husband back and the children of our community have been scarred for life by the poison this company brought to Jaguarcocha, but today is a good day for my people."

As she spoke, a black SUV drove past slowly. The passenger window opened and a man aimed his fingers at Nina in the shape of a pistol. She stared at the car as it passed and, undeterred, continued speaking. "They may attack us and even try to kill us, but they will never break our spirit. We will never stop defending the land of our ancestors."

Nina left her lawyer to take further questions and took her children to begin the long journey back home to Jaguarcocha. She did not know what the future held, but she thanked the forest gods for today.

Chapter 43

It's been a few weeks since that night on the clifftop and I'm slowly picking up the pieces of my life. I've come to an important decision: I'm going to sell the flat and move down to the coast. This flat reminds me too much of a life that will never be. Every corner of it reminds me of Christina and while I don't want to forget her, I need to be in a place where I can be free of constant triggers sending me into a depressive tailspin. Sitting on the beach that night made me realise how much I miss open spaces and sea air, and how I don't want to be in London anymore.

I've been busy sorting out the flat, carefully packing away Christina's clothes and belongings, and talking to agents about moving. It's been good to regain some measure of control over my life.

I've also told the editor I no longer want to look after the crime desk at the paper. I doubt I'll give up journalism completely because writing is in my blood, but I'd rather do it on my own terms than be beholden to whatever is hitting the news every week. I'd like to go in a more investigative direction and cover more environmental issues. I don't know in what capacity exactly, so I'm going to take time off and it will figure itself out.

I thought long and hard about covering one last story – the death of Campbell – but decided it would be better written by someone less emotionally involved. His death was reported locally in Sussex as a probable suicide, but it didn't make national news until Steve did a follow-up documenting Campbell's activities in South America and how threat of exposure may have driven him to suicide. As Steve said to me bluntly, 'Dead men can't sue'.

Steve laid out all the evidence – the mining, the threats to the Jaguarcocha community, the poisoning of indigenous leaders and, with my blessing, he mentioned Christina's death, using only her maiden name Bautista to keep my name out of it. It's the only mention of Christina by name in the media, and I felt it was fitting that Steve was the one to cover it. He included a summary of her research on local communities and environmental conflicts. I know she would be pleased the corruption she exposed finally got the coverage it deserved.

I haven't told Steve what happened on the clifftop. I haven't told anyone and doubt I ever will. I did tell Steve I'd been in touch with Campbell though. There was no point hiding that as there must be a record of my email to him, but I didn't mention our meeting or what really happened to him.

Campbell's family strongly disputed the official verdict of suicide. I tried not to read much about it. I already had mixed feelings about what happened to him and thinking of him as a family man complicated it even further. I'm not sorry he's dead, but I empathise with the family he left behind. I remind myself there was no way I could have known what Root had planned, and there was no way of stopping him either. I still have trouble getting my head around everything that happened. The drugs, the blow to the head and the stress of the situation must have affected my memory of it as well. Now I just want to move on.

Steve's report ended on an optimistic note. He did some digging and talked with Richie, discovering that since the death of Campbell, the community of Jaguarcocha has won a court case in Quito to suspend mining operations and gain compensation. I have no doubt the company will appeal but it's a battle won, even if it's a long war. Christina would have been very pleased.

If I thought I wouldn't hear from Root again though, I was wrong. A week after that night on the cliffs, I received an email from an account named 'Roottoglory' with the subject line 'Robin Hood'.

Attached to the email were several screenshots of bank accounts. I looked closely and all showed a balance of zero. The account names were Anglo-American Petrol, AD&D Timber, Inter-American

Leather and others. They were all companies of Green Shoots victims.

I presume from the Robin Hood reference that Root and his associates must have carried out a massive cyber theft, stealing millions from these companies. I wonder if they got round to giving it to the poor or just kept the money.

There were no reports of a mass hacking in the news, so I wonder if the companies even reported it or if the police chose not to disclose it for fear of emboldening other radicals. I've deliberated over whether to cover it myself, but I'm concerned it will just invite more questions from the police on how I got my information. And after all, I've resigned from the crime desk.

Something strange happened yesterday though. I received an invitation in the post for a launch event from The Green Futures Foundation. I've never heard of it but what really perplexed me was how the foundation knew my home address. All work-related invitations go to the newspaper and, with my history of run-ins with organised crime, I keep my home address closely guarded.

The invitation reads:

Dear Mr Adamson,

We know you take a keen interest in global environmental issues so we are delighted to invite you to the launch of The Green Futures Foundation.

Our foundation aims to support ecological projects

288

around the world through rewilding and reforestation, as well as through ethical investment in sustainable business and by providing legal services to local communities threatened by corporate interests.

We are holding a launch event at the DoubleTree Plaza Hotel in London at 12 p.m. on 15th May. Please join us to hear more about our projects and to thank our trustees, whose generosity has made this foundation possible.

Sincerely,

Robin Oakley, Chair

They also sent a mission statement and background on the foundation. The launch is today and the invitation has piqued my curiosity. At the end of the document is a list of trustees. I don't recognise any names but one sticks in my mind: Ruud Jäger.

Root mentioned ploughing the money he'd stolen into something positive. "Money to defend the Earth, to boost the right type of growth," he said. Could this Ruud Jäger be Root? It's a foreign name, which would explain that accent I've never been able to place. I do a few searches online on the name but nothing comes up. If it is indeed him, it's likely to be a false name anyway.

I decide to look up the name's meaning, recalling his clue about Campbell's 'crooked mouth'. Both names are Dutch. Ruud means 'famous wolf' and Jäger means 'hunter'. I don't think that's a coincidence. It seems like his predatory style.

He told me he would leave me alone as long as I left him alone. If this is indeed him, then why am I invited to this launch? Perhaps it annoyed him that I thought he was just a common thief and he wants to show me exactly what he's been doing. I admit I have a grudging respect for his motivation, if not his methods. I'm curious, so I decide to go.

I take the train into the city and arrive just before midday in the hotel conference room. It's busy. I scan the faces around the room, but I don't see anyone who looks like him.

Applause breaks out as a woman comes onto the small stage at the front. She launches into a speech highlighting key environmental problems worldwide, then outlines some projects the foundation is launching or supporting. There are rewilding land purchases in Ecuador, Colombia and Peru that will create new nature reserves. She also mentions a total of six pending court cases in which free legal aid has been offered to various indigenous communities fighting development on their land, not only in South America but also in Africa and Asia.

It's an impressive speech but I'm not listening too closely because I'm still looking around the audience. Near the front I see a woman with shoulder-length blonde hair. She briefly turns around. She looks familiar. I look closer and I don't think I'm imagining it – she looks a lot like the woman with red hair who drugged me. I recall in one of the killings there was a witness report of a woman with red hair, and at another crime scene a report of a woman with blonde hair. It may be the same woman in different wigs. I think this may be her. I try to get closer to where she's sitting, but a security official blocks my way. "I'm sorry, sir, all seats are taken. It's standing room only at the back."

If she's here, I'm betting he is too. I look around the audience again and then turn to scan people standing behind me. I see a man in a Panama hat. He turns towards me. We lock eyes for a second, he gives a half smile and turns to leave. It's him, and he's seen me.

I try to follow, but there are too many people to push past. By the time I get into the hotel lobby he's nowhere to be seen. I exit the revolving doors and look each way. I can just glimpse a man in a hat to the right. He's already a block away.

I take off after him. He turns and glances behind, but then my view is blocked by the crowd. It's a busy day and tourists are out in force. I can't see him. I keep moving and look down the side streets, but there's no sign. Then I see the Panama hat on the floor. I pick it up and dust it off. I look around again, but I've lost him.

My phone rings. Private number.

"Macavity's not there, John."

He makes a tutting sound like he's talking to a disobedient child.

"I was quite clear, John. Do not seek me out. I think you might need a little reminder of the terms of our agreement and the consequences of breaking it. Check your email."

I open email on my phone. There's a new message from 'Roottooblivion'. It has an attachment. I open it and it's a photograph. I squint at the dark image. It's Campbell and me in the car, both clearly identifiable.

"Now, John, as you recall, the police have already taken a great interest in you. I'm sure they'd be very interested to receive this photograph. They may well believe you were the last person to see Campbell alive. That might not go so well for you, John."

He's set me up with the police before. I don't doubt he'd do it again.

"Okay, you hold the cards as usual. What do you want?"

"I already told you, John. I may call on you in time, but do not seek me out or share what you know with anyone. Then these photographs will remain our little secret. As you know, I will be watching. Goodbye, John."

Chapter 44: Jäger

Ruud Jäger put his phone away and smiled. John's persistence was no surprise, and his instincts told him he should probably tie up this particular loose end, but he had a soft spot for John. Hopefully, he would heed the warning.

Things had gone even better than expected, but it was time to lie low for a while, to plant some seeds and wait before moving onto the next phase.

Standing in the middle of the pavement, he ignored the impatience of office workers trying to get past. It was a beautiful day in London, so he decided to walk back to the office.

As he approached the high-rise glass building, a small group of workers were standing outside smoking. They stopped their conversation when they saw him. One of them instinctively straightened up and took his hand out of his pocket. Jäger nodded back at them.

He walked through the revolving doors of Securicor System Services and a security guard greeted him. "Good morning, sir. How are you?"

"I'm good, thank you, Simon. Things are looking up."

"I'm glad to hear it, sir."

He headed towards the elevator and smiled to himself. "Yes. Things are definitely looking up."

Chapter 45: DCI Morrison

DCI Morrison was in her office looking through the Green Shoots case files. As far as Edmunds was concerned, the threat was gone and they had the right man in Abel Jackson.

DCI Morrison had serious doubts though. There were too many unanswered questions. Why would a killer with the skills to pull off so many killings make a rookie mistake and turn on the phone of one of the victims? And why would he leave so much evidence on his computer, having covered his tracks so well previously?

Then there was the fact that Jackson didn't fit any of the descriptions of suspects – the man with glasses in the bar with Blakely, the woman seen at Shawcross's room and the woman meeting Hennessy in the pub.

Morrison looked over the two sketches of these suspects – a man and a woman. They looked so generic, they could be anybody. That's what happens when trying to get sketches from witnesses in pubs – memories are so hazy that images are often useless.

Morrison had made her concerns about the case clear

to Edmunds and DS Harman, but Harman told her curtly, "If you want to explain to the boss that the Met should admit Jackson's death was a tragic mistake, go ahead, but on your head be it."

They hadn't closed the case, but Edmunds had been seconded elsewhere and the rest of the department, including the chief constable, thought Green Shoots was solved. After all, the killings had stopped with Jackson's death.

However, Morrison had read in the local news about the death of Charles Campbell. It struck her immediately that he fit the profile of a Green Shoots target. He was involved in mining, an industry mentioned in the first video from the killers. It was not her case though and Sussex police had ruled it a regulation suicide, but Morrison trusted her instincts that something was amiss and requested the case file.

As she read it through, the phone records caught her attention. Campbell's last text message read simply, 'Rocks'. It had been texted to 999 emergency. That was oddly familiar. She looked through Campbell's phone records in more detail and found a phone call two days before he died from a number she recognised. She checked the records. It was John Adamson's number.

Morrison drew a sharp intake of breath and sat back in her chair. "John, John… what have you been doing?"

Epilogue

"Hi, Steve. How's it going?"

"Hi, mate. All good. Listen, we're having a little party on Saturday."

"Oh, right. What's the occasion?"

"Nothing in particular – the start of summer. I had thought of calling it my 'dodging a bullet party' with Wild West fancy dress, but Alison didn't see the funny side."

"Good grief, I'm not surprised!"

"Yeah, I know. Well anyway, we'd love you to come."

"I'll think about it."

"Come on, John. I know what that means. Just say yes, will you? There'll be a few people you haven't met. A few single women too."

I laugh. "Are you trying to fix me up, Steve?"

"What if I am? What's the harm? But just come along for a few drinks, eh?"

"Okay. Will do."

"Oh, by the way, Alison heard from Jessica that

you've been keeping regular appointments. That's good to hear."

"Yeah, I think you were right. Therapy seems to be helping, so I'm giving it a go for a while."

"Good to hear, mate. Keep at it. Listen, one p.m. Saturday, okay? It's a barbecue so bring a bottle and something to grill. No beef though, as it's banned in our house now. Gotta go!"

"Okay, see you then."

I'm in a park in Hove, close to my new flat. I remember we came here once for the weekend. You loved Brighton and said we should consider moving here. I finally decided to take your advice. It's a beautiful place and being by the sea gives me a feeling of freedom I never had in London.

I shall wear white flannel trousers and walk upon the beach.

It's a new start for me here. A place where I can try to focus on the future. I even got myself a cat – a ginger mog I've named Marmalade. He's gorgeous but a right little rascal. He keeps bringing in mice and leaving them on the doormat, as if he's bringing me breakfast. You would laugh, or scream. Maybe both.

I'm in a garden square with a flowerbed in the centre, framed by thick hedges. I chose this secluded spot for your memorial bench. The park is often quite busy, but there's nobody in this corner. It's a relief because I want to talk to you without worrying about people thinking I'm crazy. I always find it comforting to talk to you.

298

I walk to the far side of the square to your bench and sit down. The inscription reads:

In memory of Christina Bautista Adamson (1988–2021), loving wife and defender of the forest.

It's the 6th of June, the anniversary of the day we first met. Every year, I'm going to come here and remember that day in the thermal baths in the highlands of Ecuador. It was a perfect day and it always will be.

I'm so glad I met you, mi amor. You showed me it was possible to fall in love and that feeling will never leave me. I may not be a religious man, but if there is a God, then he sent me an angel. You will always be my angel.

I've learnt so much over the past few months – about your work and about what's really important in life.

You were right too about there being enough heaven on Earth to enjoy. Like Hemingway said, it is worth fighting for.

I'm not ready to leave this world. I have more work to do and I'm going to dedicate my life from now on to fighting for what you believed in.

Maybe one day I will learn to love again but I'm not ready yet. I hope you'll understand if one day I am ready.

Steve invited me to a party this weekend. I think I should go and enjoy myself, don't you?

I was thinking about what you wrote in your last

email to me, about how we could think of each other at the same time to feel closer to one other. I love that idea and I know wherever you are, you are here with me now.

I wrote something for you. I hope you like it

> *You are here,*
> *We're never apart,*
> *Have no fear,*
> *Because I am in your heart,*
> *As you are in mine,*
> *We are forever entwined.*

> *I let my thoughts fly,*
> *High into the sky,*
> *There our hearts will meet,*
> *In a moment so sweet,*
> *Then I will know,*
> *That you didn't really go,*
> *For we are in each other's hearts forever.*

I open the urn and scatter the ashes on the grass around the bench. Beneath the ashes, I can see green shoots peeking through.

Acknowledgements

I would like to thank the following people who provided information and inspiration to help me write this book. In Ecuador, Bethany Pitts, Holmer Machoa, Nina Gualinga, Andres Tapia and Jeff Frazier. In the UK, the fantastic publishing team at Cranthorpe Millner, as well as tutors Martin Ouvry from City University, and Andrew Hurley and Lisa O'Donnell from Curtis Brown Creative. To T.S. Eliot, whose wonderful poem *The Love Song of J. Alfred Prufrock* is quoted several times in the book. Finally, thanks to my family – my beloved late wife Carolina, my children Jake and Isabella, my parents John and Louise, and my sister Lucinda.

To accompany the release of his debut novel, Ben is releasing a Green Shoots Soundtrack of ten original songs on the themes of grief, loss, love and healing, available on Spotify, iTunes and all major music channels from September 2022. For further information on Ben's music, visit benwestwoodmusic.com or benwestwood.net.